Having tried a variety of careers in retail, marketing and nursing, **Louisa George** is thrilled that her dream job of writing for Mills & Boon means she gets to go to work in her pyjamas. Louisa lives in Auckland, New Zealand, with her husband, two sons and two male cats. When not writing or reading Louisa loves to spend time with her family, enjoys travelling, and adores eating great food.

REUNITED
BY THEIR
SECRET SON

LOUISA GEORGE

MILLS & BOON

First published in Great Britain 2018
by Mills & Boon, an imprint of HarperCollins*Publishers*
1 London Bridge Street, London, SE1 9GF

Large Print edition 2018

ISBN: 978-0-263-07308-9

MIX
Paper from
responsible sources
FSC® C007454

CHAPTER ONE

HE WAS LATE.

Finn Baird was never late—not any more. These days he always gave himself extra time to navigate the traffic, negotiate the car park and be in his clinic with plenty of minutes to spare. Mainly so he could both impress the boss and be mentally prepared for the day. But also so he could make readjustments to his leg before he started work.

He just hadn't anticipated the readjustments would take so long today. Or hurt so damned much.

Which was more than a little irritating because now he was rushing, and the more he rushed the slower he seemed to get, not to mention the more frustrated.

Two months into his new job as paediatric physiotherapist at St Margaret's Children's Hospital—Maggie's to the locals—and he'd made sure he had a reputation for having all the time in the world for his patients. Hell, they deserved it. A lot of them had challenges worse than his and most of them grinned their way through treatment. Through all the pulling and pushing and straightening and bending he made them do, through all the pain, through all the mind-numbingly repetitive exercises, he tried to make them laugh. Tried to make them believe they could achieve anything if they tried.

He definitely needed to take a leaf out of their books.

Trying to smile and hurry along the corridor while gritting his teeth against the pain, he reached the reception area at the same time his boss did. Neither of them looked at their watches. Neither of them acknowledged Finn was late.

And hell, if that was preferential treatment he didn't want it. 'Sorry I'm late, Ross. Won't happen again.'

'Good morning, Finn. Don't worry; I know you'll make it up.' Ross Andrews, Head of Physiotherapy, threw a pile of paper folders onto the reception desk and looked up. 'You always stay later than everyone else anyway.'

Because he needed to stay on top of everything. Needed this job to work out, and everything took longer these days. 'Just want to get the job done properly.'

'And you do. So you're forgiven for being a few minutes behind. Great run yesterday. Feeling it a bit today? I certainly am. I think I twinged my back.' Ross put his palms on the small of his back and stretched backwards. 'I've got to fix that overpronation.'

'You want me to take a look?'

'Later, if we get a chance. One of the perks of being a physio, eh? Treatment on tap. I'm so impressed with your race time, Finn—you did great. Really great.'

The minutes were ticking by but Finn could hardly snap at the boss and head to his first patient, so he took a deep breath and promised himself he'd be doubly efficient today without hurrying the littlies.

'Let's be honest—I ran a woeful time. I'm just glad I made it to the finish line.' There had been a time when he'd completed the ten-mile Great

Edinburgh Run in under an hour; this time he'd been lucky—and utterly exhausted and hurting on both his good leg and his gone one—to finish half the distance in the same time. He rubbed his left thigh, still sore and tight, but nowhere near as painful as just below his knee where the stitches had been and where the friction was always most intense. 'Still, I stayed upright—that was a bonus. I'm aiming for a faster time next year.'

'Don't push yourself too hard—you'll get there. You just need a little incentive…if you know what I mean. Someone to run towards.' Ross's eyes grew wider as he nodded.

Finn grinned, remembering seeing Ross overtake him on the home straight, having run twice the distance, right into the arms of his new wife. She'd been so proud of him even Finn hadn't been able to stop smiling as she cheered and screamed her husband's name as he went over the finishing line. And then there'd been the kisses; the poor man had barely been able to catch breath.

'A special someone to cheer me on at the end,

right? I'm going to be running a long, long way before that ever happens.'

His boss laughed. 'Well, you'll never have it if you don't even ask a lassie out. Greta's sister said to drop a huge hint about a double date. She's single too—?'

Ugh. Not another date set-up. He was starting to regret getting to know his boss a little better out of work. Seemed Finn was surrounded by loved-up couples these days who wanted him to have a piece of the happiness they had. If it wasn't Ross and Greta it was his brother Callum and his new family down in New Zealand dropping hints at every available opportunity about seeing him paired up. The thing none of them understood—or downright ignored—was the issue of his leg. Or lack of it. If he'd struggled to come to terms with it, then what chance did any woman have? How could he give them what they wanted? 'Thanks, but no. Really, no.'

Ross shook his head, undeterred as a matchmaker. 'I never understood why you turned down lovely Julia, the Pilates instructor. Or Molly-Rae from the café…she was definitely dropping big hints to go for a drink. Even I could see that.'

Finn dug deep to keep polite. He dredged up a smile. 'I mean it, boss. No.'

'Or there's the speed dating night every Thursday at the Tavern?' Ross shrugged. 'A bit lame, I know. But it's always a laugh. I went there a few times before I met Greta. As you know, we met at salsa night—oh. Well… Yes…' He glanced at Finn's leg and shrugged again. 'If you can run, you can dance.'

Dancing was a whole lot more than just moving forward in a straight line. 'Really. I'm fine. Thanks. I'm not looking for anyone. Please tell the lovely Greta I'm fine on my own.'

Even as he said it he knew it sounded hollow. But there it was. Before the accident, Finn had taken his looks and raw physicality for granted and enjoyed them, celebrated them with the best and the most beautiful women he could find. He'd paraded around like a prize chump, all cocky and sure of himself, a peacock on show. He'd had a host of women who'd wanted what he'd wanted: a night of fun and drink and mindless sex. Then his charmed life had started to unravel and the last thing he'd wanted was to attempt dating again. Couldn't do it, but it didn't stop them asking. Or his friends trying to set him up.

Most of those women were a blur to him now. All except one…the one who'd not got away, not exactly. The one he'd purposefully let go after he'd fallen from grace, fallen from a great bloody height and broken both his dreams and his body.

Now? He didn't need anyone. Didn't want anyone. Didn't want anyone to see him like this, not after who he'd been before. Not after he'd changed so damned much he was barely recognisable inside or out. 'If I change my mind, Ross, you'll be the first to know.'

'Aye, well, I was like you once—thought I was better off being a lad—but there comes a time in every man's life when he has to settle down. Get serious.'

'I've a long way before I go to those extremes.' Finn laughed. 'I'm pretty serious about myself these days and that's about all I can manage for now.' He'd had to relearn how to do pretty much everything and was still learning. He changed the subject, jumping into work as always. Because work made him focus on the possible, not the impossible, like having a woman who even liked the look of him, let alone could fall for him and see a future. 'I'm going to be running very late, so I need to get on. Who've we got today?'

'Some regular follow-ups from your predecessor and a couple of new referrals. Nothing too taxing. You're doing just fine. Don't rush. They'll understand.' Ross looked meaningfully again at Finn's left leg.

'I prefer it if the leg doesn't come up in conversation.' Finn whipped round to peer at the computer for details of his first client, twisting his leg in the prosthetic. A searing pain ran up his knee. He inhaled sharply, clenched his teeth and waited for the pain to subside. 'Okay. Okay. Let's go.'

'You all right? You need a seat?' Reaching out to steady Finn, Ross peered at him, all concern and questions.

Damn. The last thing he needed was a father figure…scratch that, a *brother* figure. He already had one of those and even twelve thousand miles away he still managed to be overbearing and overly concerned about Finn's welfare. All. The. Time.

The whole point of taking this job and being this new person in a new city, putting the past well and truly behind him, was to live a normal life. He didn't want people to keep asking if he was all right. And yes, he knew they cared and were just being nice. But he didn't want to be treated any differently to everyone else.

He counted to ten under his breath as the pain faded. 'Yep. I'm fine. But even after more than two years I keep forgetting.' And it wasn't just the physical pain that assailed him, sometimes out of nowhere. 'Still, I'm good to go. And now I'm really late.'

Four hours later and his leg was no better, neither was his mood, although the kids always made him smile. A missed appointment meant he could catch up. All he had to do now was finish these notes and then he could lock his door, slip off his prosthesis and the silicone liner and relax for a few minutes.

As he sat in his office—the closest to Reception so he wouldn't have to walk far, apparently—he heard a kerfuffle in the waiting area.

A woman's voice, soft and apologetic. Breathless. 'I'm so, so late. I'm sorry. Really sorry. Lachie had a meltdown at home which delayed things a bit…you know what it's like…he's hit the terrible twos six months early. Then I couldn't get a parking space and then there was something wrong with the pushchair—I think it might be one of the front wheels; it's wanting to go in the opposite direction to all the others.'

The talking stopped. Finn assumed it was for the woman to draw breath. He heard the receptionist sigh. Then that soft voice again. 'I know you're all busy. I'm so sorry. Please, if anyone could see us I'm happy to wait as long as it takes.'

Their receptionist was renowned for running a tight ship. 'I'm sorry but we have a full list today and there's no wriggle room to fit you in. I can make another appointment for Lachie?'

'He really needs to be seen today. I know it's not relevant, or shouldn't be, but I've taken the day off work as holiday just so we could get here. I'm fast running out of holiday days…' Desperation laced her words. 'It's his boots, you see—they're rubbing and he hates wearing them. That was the trouble this morning—when

I took them off after he'd worn them all night he threw them across the room.' A pause. 'Please.'

Finn stretched his left knee. Yeah, he knew all about rubbing. About the tension before you put the damned thing on because you just knew it was going to be sore. He knew how hard that was for a grown man to get his head round, never mind a…what did she say?…eighteen-month-old. He sent an urgent message to the receptionist's screen.

I'll see them. Just give me a few minutes to finish these notes.

A message flicked back:

Thanks. The good karma fairy is looking down on you.

'Okay. One of the physiotherapists will miss his lunch for you. Please take a seat.'

The softly spoken woman's voice wavered. 'Oh. That's very kind. Thank you. Thank you. Lachie? The nice man will see you soon.'

Finn walked through to the waiting room and was just about to call out the boy's name when he was struck completely dumb. His heart thudded against his ribcage as he watched the woman reading a story to her child. Her voice quiet and sing-song, dark hair tumbling over one shoulder, ivory skin. A gentle manner. Soft.

His brain rewound, flickering like an old film reel: dark curls on the pillow. Warm caramel eyes. A mouth that tasted so sweet. Laughter in the face of grief. One night.

That night…

A lifetime ago.

He snapped back to reality. He wasn't that man any more; he'd do well to remember that. He cleared his throat and glanced down at the notes file in his hand to remind himself of the name. 'Lachlan Harding?'

'Yes. Yes—oh?' She froze, completely taken aback. For a second he saw fear flicker across her eyes then she stood up. Fear? Why? Because he'd never called as he'd promised? 'Finn? Is it you? It's Finn, yes?'

There was little warmth there; her mouth was taut in a straight line. No laughter. Not at all. She was still startlingly pretty. Not a trace of make-up, but she didn't need anything to make her any more beautiful. His gut clenched as he remembered more of that night and how good she'd made him feel.

Too bad, matey.

The fear gone, she smiled hesitantly and tugged the boy closer to her leg, her voice a little wobbly and a little less soft. 'Wow. Finn, this is a surprise—'

'Sophie. Hello. Yes, I'm Finn. Long time, no see.' Glib, he knew, when there was so much he should say to explain what had happened, why he hadn't called, but telling her his excuses during a professional consultation wasn't the right time. Besides, she had a child now; she'd moved on from their one night together, clearly. He glanced at her left hand, the one that held her boy so close—no wedding ring. But that didn't mean a thing these days; she could be happily unmarried and in a relationship.

And why her marital status pinged into his head he just didn't know. He had no right to wonder after the silence he'd held for well over two years.

They were just two people who'd shared one night a long time ago. There was no professional line to cross here. He was doing her a favour by seeing her son. If things felt awkward he could always assign her to a different physiotherapist for the next appointment.

'Yes. Wow. It's a small world.' He infused his manner with professionalism, choosing not to go down Memory Lane. He was a different man now. Although he couldn't help but notice as he turned that his left leg was shaking a little more than usual. In fact, all of him was. It was surprise, that was all. His past life clashing with his present. He concentrated hard on being steady and not limping in front of her, because for some reason it mattered that she saw him as whole. 'Right, then, so this is Lachie? Come on through.'

Good karma? No chance. Judging by the way Sophie was looking at him, the good karma fairy had gone on her lunch break.

Finn.

Wow.

Sophie put her hand to her mouth and followed him into the examination room. Tried to act calm while her heart hammered against her chest wall. So many questions.

Finn. She hadn't even known his surname. *Geez.* It was on his badge. Finn Baird. That information would have been immensely useful a few years ago.

Wow. Here he was, after all this time. After everything. She gaped at him, wanting to rail at him, to put her fists on his chest and pound. Hard. Wanted to ask him where the hell he'd been and what the hell he'd been doing. But she did none of that and instead she smiled, fussed around her son and pretended being here with the man who'd no doubt forgotten her the moment she'd left the hotel room was no big deal at all.

The most important person in the room was Lachie, so both she and Finn needed to rise above any failed promises from a long time ago. 'This is Lachie. He's eighteen months old. He's got bilateral talipes. He's been treated with the Ponseti method and now we're just keeping the feet straight with boots and bars at night.' She paused and tried not to sound as rattled as she felt. 'Thanks for fitting us in. I'm sorry we missed our appointment with Ross.'

'He's got a meeting across town, otherwise I'm

sure he'd have waited for you.' *Oh. Okay. So no chance of a reprieve, then.*

Finn lifted his eyes from Lachie's notes and met her gaze. She couldn't tell in those Celtic blue irises what the hell was going on in his head, but she knew by the complete lack of concern in his demeanour that he had no idea. No idea at all.

'So this is his routine check-up? How's he doing with the boots and bars?'

'Not well, I'm afraid. He's pretty grumpy about it all.' She picked her son up and popped him on the examination couch and tickled him. Pretty much guaranteed to bring a smile to his face. Because right now she couldn't cope with another tantrum. Right now she wanted to rewind the clock to this morning, have a different start to the day and make her appointment with the other physiotherapist on time. 'Grumpy, aren't you? Mr Monster?'

Her boy threw his head back and giggled. It was such a delicious sound and always made her world a lot better when she heard it. She looked over and saw Finn watching her. Was he doing the maths?

Her heart contracted in a swift and urgent need to protect her boy. She put her arms around him and held him close. But Finn seemed completely oblivious to what was right in front of his face. 'You're still working, Sophie? I heard you say something about it at Reception. A nurse—that's right?'

So he'd remembered that at least. Had he remembered anything else? How right it had felt? How crazy it had been to find someone who *got* you in a city the size of Edinburgh, a country the size of Scotland? That was what she'd thought then. Now she could only think of curse words. She bit them back. 'Yes. I'm a Health Visitor now, though. I work out of Campbell Street clinic.'

'Ah. A nine-to-five gig?'

'More like eight until eight most days. But yes.'

'You like it?'

What did it matter to him? What did any of her life matter to him?

It was hard to believe she was here having a conversation about minor stuff instead of the conversation they should have been having. But not here, not in front of Lachie. 'I don't want to take up more of your time than I should. Let's get on, shall we? It's all in the notes but I'll précis for you. It'll be quicker. Lachie had eight castings to make his feet straight and a tenotomy to loosen the heel cords, which hurt but he tolerated. He wears the boots and bars only at night-time and for his afternoon naps now. I try to make sure he has them on close to twelve hours a day.' She took the offending plastic boots out of her bag and gave them to Finn. 'He hates them.'

Finn's eyes widened but he nodded. If he was rattled by her he didn't show it, at least not to Lachie. For that she was grateful. Finn grinned down at the boy. 'So, Mr Monster, eh? Cool name, buddy. The rest of us get stuck with boring ones like Finn. That's me. Finn.' He stuck his hand out towards Lachie, who was staring up at him with his wide—Celtic blue—eyes. 'You want to shake hands? No? How about a high five? That's right, my man. High. Low…' Finn brought his hand up high then down low then right back to meet Lachie's little palm. 'Ah, you got me. You're too quick.' He looked down at

Lachie's feet and asked, 'Is it okay if I look at your feet? Can you take your trainers off? Atta boy.'

Sophie's heart was bursting with pride as she watched Lachie rip the Velcro on his trainers with a huge grin. Then even more as he hit them on the examination trolley until they flashed. 'Flash.'

'Whoa.' Finn raised his palms and looked very impressed. 'This is superhero territory.'

He leaned his hips against the couch and stamped his right foot. Then wobbled minutely and grabbed the gurney, glancing for the tiniest of moments over to Sophie and then back at Lachie. Which was a little strange.

Was he checking if she'd seen him wobble? Or just checking if she was watching his examination? Some health professionals were spooked if they had to treat other medics, in case they were being judged.

Finn shrugged. 'See? Mine don't flash at all. I need a pair of those. If only you could wear the flashing ones at night instead, eh? But they are for daytime adventures and these...' he picked up the clinical plastic boots and showed them to

Lachie '…these are for night-time adventures. I know, I know you don't like them but they'll give you even more superhero powers if you keep them on. Right, let's have a look at those toes. Ten? You have ten toes? Excellent. I won't tickle, I promise. Well, not if you don't want me to.'

'Can you see the redness?' She knew she was starting to sound rude but being in here was suffocating. The pride in her son mingled with sadness and anger in Sophie's chest. Finn should have called as he'd said he would. He should have damned well called. She tried to hurry him up. 'There, at the back of the heel.'

'Well, the feet are nice and straight so that's good. But yes, there is some redness. The boots seem to be the right size. Have you tried putting Vaseline in? That helps.'

'Yes. But he's so wriggly when I put them on it's like a game of Twister, all arms and legs. I think he's scraping his heels against the plastic when he tries to scramble his feet out while I try to squeeze them in.'

Finn nodded. 'Yes, it's a common problem. I'll give you some second skin plasters; they should help. It's often easier to have someone else around to give you a hand putting the boots on at bedtime. Either that or become an octopus.'

'An octopus?'

'Eight arms.' He grinned at his little joke.

She didn't. 'Well, we'll just have to manage because...' She didn't want to say it, not to him, but it was the truth. She'd lost her beloved grandmother—her main cheerleader her whole life—before she'd even met Finn. Her parents had barely been in the same hemisphere as her for twenty-odd years. And she'd been too busy being a working single mum to raise her head over the dating parapet. '... There is no one else.'

Finn's head shot up from examining Lachie. 'I see. Okay. Well, listen, Mr Monster, could you be a good boy and sit very still when your Mummy puts your boots on every night?'

Lachie nodded, open-mouthed.

'I've got some superhero stickers for you. Every time you sit still for Mummy you can have a sticker. Deal? And you can put them on your night-time boots and make them fit for a superhero like you.'

'Yes.' Lachie nodded and laughed. 'Dickers.'

'Stickers, honey. St…stickers. Thanks, er, Finn. That's a great idea. We'll try them.'

Typical. Every night was a battleground lately and, no matter what she'd done or said or promised, Lachie had fought her about those boots. Now he was nodding, all big-eyed at Finn.

Yes, life would have been immensely easier if there'd been two pairs of hands throughout her pregnancy and the birth and the endless hospital appointments for Lachie's feet. Two parents to ease the strain. Two brains to work out how to deal with his problems and work out a shared timetable instead of it all being on her, juggling everything. Two hearts to love him. Because he deserved that, more than anything.

She pressed her lips together and stopped a stream of bad words escaping her mouth. At least the man was taking time out of his schedule to see them. He wasn't all bad.

There had been many times, usually during one of Lachie's sleepless nights, or more recently during his tantrums, when she'd thought the opposite. She really needed to talk to him.

Finn grinned. 'Let's see you walking, shall we? Just bare feet.'

'He started to walk at fourteen months, and he's met all his other milestones. I had him treated as soon as we could and I've been pedantic about making sure he's wearing the boots and bars. The staff at Nursery know what to do and snap the bars on every nap time too.' She looked at the thin plastic boots and the metal bar they snapped into to hold his feet at the correct angle, for over half of his short life, and her heart pinged again. It hadn't been plain sailing.

'Well, it's definitely working. Look, the feet are just a little splayed out and that's what we want for now. Perfect.' Well, the guy definitely knew his stuff; she couldn't fault him on that. Finn lifted Lachie to the floor then he walked to the far end of the room.

Interesting. He definitely favoured his left leg as he walked. A subtle limp he hadn't had that night. Knowing him, it was a rugby injury; he'd mentioned he played. That had accounted for the body she'd enjoyed so damned much. She watched him now, the way he moved with less finesse but with a body that sung with the benefits of hard-core exercise. Beneath his navy polo shirt she saw the outline of muscles, the hug of short sleeves around impeccable biceps. His perfect backside in those black trousers. Her stomach contracted at the thought of what they'd done in that hotel room, the way he'd treated her with reverence, the way he'd slowly undressed her and caressed her. The taste of him.

She swallowed hard and pushed a rare rush of lust away. She had no right thinking like that. He'd let her down. Let her son down.

She appraised the simple facts; he was a man who knew a lot about keeping a body fit, that was all. A physiotherapy student, he'd said he was, and a rugby player for some club or other; she hadn't ever followed the sport so it had meant nothing to her.

Knowing him. Well, she didn't, did she? Not at all. She'd liked him. A lot. They'd clicked. At least she'd thought so.

Turned out they hadn't. When he didn't call she'd tried to find him but it was hard to find someone when you didn't know their surname. She'd Googled. Scoured social media. Even checked out the physiotherapy departments in every Scottish university, but he'd disappeared into thin air and in the end she'd had to give up.

The guy really hadn't wanted to know her at all. Or her child.

His child.

CHAPTER TWO

THERE IS NO one else.

Sophie's words had been going over and over in his head since the consultation yesterday. No ring. No partner. And each time she'd appeared in his brain his gut had jumped at the thought of her being single, then taken a dive as he registered the reality of his situation.

But something was bugging him about the boy and her story, like a jigsaw puzzle piece that didn't fit. He couldn't put a finger on it, but her demeanour had been off. She'd been in a hurry to leave. She'd kept the boy close. As if…as if what? As if she didn't trust Finn with him. Why the hell not?

Shaking his head, he punched the boy's name into his work computer and waited for Lachie's file to appear.

'Hey. Put the work down. It's past six and I'm parched.' Ross appeared in the doorway to Finn's office, briefcase in hand and coat on. 'Fancy a drink at the Tavern? I'm meeting Greta and some of the gang from here are coming down too.'

Oh-oh, that spelt trouble. 'It's not some sort of blind date thing, is it?'

'You really are dating-shy, aren't you?' Ross was all pretend offended as he put his hand on his heart. 'Would I do that to you?'

'I don't know.' Finn thought back to yesterday's conversation. 'Yes. Probably.'

'I can one hundred per cent assure you that I have not arranged for any single women to be in the vicinity of the bar tonight. Although I can't vouch for Greta; she's a different kettle of fish altogether, she's keen to see you settled. But not tonight, I promise. All I can offer is beer, maybe some greasy chips and a steak pie. Come on. You missed the last team night out.'

Because he'd been new to the job and hadn't wanted to answer a zillion questions about the accident. But, with a sigh, Finn relented. It was about time he started to extend a hand of friendship to his colleagues. If this new life was going to work out it would have to involve social stuff too. 'Sure, I'll come over when I'm done here.'

Ross walked into the office and looked over Finn's shoulder. 'Problem?'

Searching for Lachie was veering on the personal and not suitable for work. He'd have to look tomorrow to try to solve the puzzle. 'No. Just checking I wrote the notes on an extra I saw yesterday.'

Ross squinted at the screen. 'Ah, little Lachie Harding. Good kid. Mum's pretty cool too. She's worked hard with him. I wish every parent was like that. Although she missed her appointment yesterday, which isn't like her. I wondered if she turned up eventually. You saw them?'

'Yes. He's doing fine, but the boots are rubbing. I think he's getting to the age where he wants what he wants and makes sure everyone knows about it. We talked through some remedies.' Why he had such an interest in the boy he didn't want to admit. He certainly couldn't tell his boss.

I had a one-night stand. I liked her. A lot. I thought there could be something, but then

I couldn't get over my big, fat, broken ego to call her.

He had a sudden thought which made his gut plummet. What was Lachie's date of birth again? Finn had been too bamboozled seeing her again he hadn't taken much else in.

Hot damn. The boy was eighteen months old, if he remembered correctly.

Which meant he'd been born... Finn did some maths and inhaled sharply.

They'd used a condom. Hadn't they?

Of course they had. He always did.

His head started to buzz with questions as he tried to clinically reimagine what they'd done that night. But, since the accident, events from around that time were very hazy.

'Earth to Finn.' Ross tapped his foot. 'Come on, beer awaits. Get a move on.'

'Sure. I'll just grab my stuff.' Finn slung his messenger bag over his shoulder then grabbed his stick and leaned heavily on it to stand up. Ross was just about the only person he could do this in front of, even if it smacked of weakness. When he'd applied for the job he'd had to be upfront about what he was capable of and what he couldn't do, but Ross had taken him on with no hesitation.

'Still sore?' Ross glanced down at Finn's leg, taking his role as mentor and supporter very seriously.

Finn shrugged as the pain subsided. What he needed was real time off the stump. 'Just aching after the race. Nothing to worry about. I just thought I'd take a bit of pressure off with this.' He waved the folding black stick with a carved Maori *tiki* handle his brother had sent from New Zealand.

'I thought you hated using it.'

'I do.' Because it made him feel less. Made him look different to other guys his age. And yes, he was all for standing up for diversity issues, but it didn't mean he had to like the fact he only had one leg, or flaunt it, and he definitely never expected to be treated any differently to anyone else. 'Don't think for a minute it gives you an excuse to start being nice to me.'

Ross shrugged. 'Okay. Well, the last one to the pub gets the first round. And if you're going to be all equal opportunities then I'm not giving you a head start. Better get yer hand in your pocket.'

'That's right. Exploit the disabled, why don't you?' Finn laughed, glad to be treated as nothing unusual, and hurried after his boss, letting the stick take the strain for once. He'd hide it away in his bag just before they hit the pub.

Edinburgh was starting to thaw after a long cold winter but the air was still tinged with the promise of snow as they stepped outside. Finn inhaled deeply and walked down the ramp to George Street. This was good. Yes. Beers with friends. A little like old times. He smiled to himself...almost the same and yet a million times different.

Worry crept under his skin, pushing aside the smile, as his mind bounced back to Sophie. They'd used a condom. Right?

It couldn't...he couldn't...the boy. Surely not?

Not now. Not when he could barely look after himself. Not when this new life of his was hard enough to deal with.

'Finn?' A voice from the shadows of the hospital entrance made him jump.

He whirled around, almost losing his footing,

but leaned more on the stick to right himself.
'Hello?'

'Finn. It's me, Sophie.' She stepped out from
behind a huge stone pillar. Her eyes were
haunted. Her skin completely devoid of colour
as her top teeth worried her bottom lip. She had
a thick red scarf tied under her chin and tucked
into a long dark coat but, despite the layers, she
looked frozen through. For the briefest moment
he thought about wrapping his arms around her
to warm her up. Then he remembered his leg.
Remembered he'd let her down by disappearing
without a trace and not living up to his promise to call her. The likelihood of her wanting his
arms around her was less than zero per cent.

Idiot.

He glanced at Ross up ahead, just about to disappear round a corner and oblivious to Sophie's
presence, thought about calling after him in case
she wanted to chat about her son's issues, but
she'd said *Finn*. Not Ross.

In another life he'd have been flattered to have
a beautiful woman accosting him as he stepped
out of work, but she'd seen him with his stick
and his limp and they had a history. His stom-

ach tightened. *Damn. Damn. Damn.* Not a great start. But he had a feeling, judging by the way she was looking at him, things were only going to get worse.

'Hey, there. Are you okay, Sophie? You look… upset.'

She shook her head, eyes brimming with tears. 'No, I'm not okay. I can't stop thinking about it and I need to talk to you.'

Thinking about what? He tried to stay calm but the thunder in his chest kept rumbling. 'Sure. Of course. Here?'

'No. Somewhere warm.' She looked down at his stick and her eyes widened. 'Are you okay to walk? What happened?'

'I'm fine.' He felt exposed and caught off guard as he flicked the stick into thirds and shoved it in his bag. Now she'd see him as something less too. 'There's a bar across the way. Or the café in the hospital?'

'Whatever's nearer. I can't be long; I had to get a friend to watch over Lachie while I came here.'

He walked back up the ramp and inside the hospital, his heart now thundering almost out of his chest. 'Coffee?' Banal but necessary. Anything to fill the void in the conversation.

She almost flinched at his question. 'No. Thanks. Just water.'

After a few minutes they were facing each other in an otherwise empty café. Outside, the street lights cast an eerie glow. Inside, the strip lights were too bright, too clinical. He wrapped his hands around his mug of steaming coffee, bracing himself for what he'd already worked out. At least he thought he had. It was hardly rocket science. Just a bit of sex and some maths.

Only it hadn't been just sex; it had been mind-blowing. Intimate. The most intense, the most sensual he'd ever had, and he would have called her if he'd ever stopped feeling sorry for himself. 'Okay, Sophie, I'm guessing this is more than just a telling-off for not calling you?'

She nodded. 'I wish it were that simple. Believe me, I can most definitely deal with rejection and I would have chalked you up to experience and forgotten all about it.'

He guessed that was supposed to hurt him. Surprisingly, it did, a little. 'But…?'

'That night… I thought… I thought you were

okay, you know? I thought we might, well, at least see each other again. You certainly seemed keen. But you just went cold. Was I just a one-night stand to you? Was that it? Because that's not what you said at the time. That's not how it felt. But then, I was pretty cut up about my grandmother's death, so I was easy prey to someone like you.'

Ouch. Someone like you. He didn't know exactly what she meant by that but he could see how it would have looked to her: single guy picks up grieving beautiful woman. Takes advantage. Doesn't call. 'It wasn't like that. I liked you. It was...' Special. Different.

'What was it, Finn? To you?' She twisted her hands together and took a deep breath. Her nostrils flared and her jaw tightened and the deep breathing didn't seem to be helping. She looked up at him and glared. 'Whatever. Forget it. It doesn't matter now; what you felt doesn't matter. Except... Actually, you know what? I'm so angry at you because everything could have been a damned sight easier if you'd just picked up the phone.'

'I lost it. Down a mountain.' Along with his

self-esteem, his stupid decision-making and, for a long time, his positivity. Thankfully that was clawing its way back.

He wasn't going to tell her that he'd left his phone down there on purpose, that he'd made sure all his contacts were erased. That the ones in the Cloud were too. That he'd drawn a line between before the accident and after and given his brother instructions to hide as much information about Finn as he could from everyone.

Her eyebrows rose as if to say *lame excuse*. 'You know, I've thought about what I was going to say to you, so many times. I've rehearsed it over and over and now I'm here I don't actually know what to say.'

She was hurting and he didn't think it was from rejection; it was from those hard years of being pregnant and a single mother. He took a breath and jumped. 'Lachie's my son. Right?'

He prayed she was going to say *Wrong*. But why the heck else was she here? She wouldn't come this far just to berate him for not following up on a date almost two and a half years ago.

She gasped. 'I tried to find you. So hard you wouldn't believe. I always wanted you to know.

It's your right, and his. But now…' Her eyes darkened. 'I don't know what it's going to mean to you—what *he's* going to mean to you—so I don't want you to know because you might go cold again and he doesn't deserve that. He deserves a father who wants to know him, who's interested and in it for the long haul and I'm not sure you're that guy.'

Wow.

She continued, 'But you have to know, everyone says so, and I feel like I have to tell you, otherwise it's on my conscience. So, yes, my gorgeous little Lachlan Spencer Harding, that beautiful, funny, clever handful, is your son.'

Finn closed his eyes and tried to control the emotions, ones he wasn't prepared for, tumbling through him. He didn't want to be a father. He didn't want to have the responsibility of it all. He wasn't ready. Would he ever be ready? He had one leg, damn it. He could barely walk. He couldn't turn round quickly and catch a falling child. He couldn't teach him how to kick a ball or run around in the park like he'd dreamed his own dad would do, but never did. He couldn't protect himself from hurt, never mind an eighteen-month-old.

He wished they'd never had that night. He wished he'd kept in touch with her. He wished he hadn't fallen hundreds of feet down a mountain in a blizzard and made himself an invalid when now...now he needed two legs more than ever in his whole life.

He nodded, feeling the same kind of sensation he'd had that wintry night when he'd stepped into thin air...as if he was falling into a nightmare. And yet, cushioning the landing, was a bright shining kernel of something good. He had a son.

Whoa.

A giggling, wriggling superhero with two club feet who most definitely deserved the very best of fathers.

He'd had a son for one and a half years. He'd missed so much already.

And he knew all about being that kid with no dad. About the dreams of him turning up one day and being like some sort of king. About watching the other kids get to play, work, laugh with their fathers and wonder what you'd done that was so bad yours didn't want to know you. He knew how that felt and he wasn't going to let his son go through that.

He opened his eyes and looked at Sophie, who was watching him with a hand pressed to her mouth and a frown on her forehead. God knew what she'd been through. He imagined the names she'd called him. Imagined the sleepless nights, the endless worry. Then the righteous anger at his silence. It was time to man up. 'I'm so sorry.'

'Sorry?' Sophie was lost for words. She'd expected him to deny his child, demand a paternity test or be angry that she'd come here and told him. She hadn't expected this. Was it a trick?

'Yeah. I blew it. I messed up. I should have called but...' He ran a hand across his dark hair and shrugged. 'Circumstances meant I wasn't in a position to call for a while. Then I just thought... Well, to be honest, I didn't think at all.'

'Clearly. You lost your phone down a mountain, but you can retrieve information from backup online; everyone knows that.' She had nowhere to focus the anger she'd stored up for so long and he was stripping it away from her with one word. *Sorry.* It seemed as if he really was, but it wasn't enough. 'There are lots of ways to find information if you want it badly enough.' Although wanting hadn't helped her.

'I couldn't. I just couldn't, okay? I didn't know you needed me. And, if I remember rightly, the name you'd tapped into the phone was Sexy Sophie so I couldn't have looked for you anyway. We didn't do the surname thing.'

'Yes, well, I presumed we'd get to that on the second date.'

He'd said she was beautiful, called her sexy as hell, and she'd laughed and told him he was clearly drunk. But he hadn't been and neither had she. He'd been funny and caring and enigmatic. He'd stroked her back when she'd cried about her grandmother. He'd listened when she'd told him about the hole in her life without her and he'd told her about how cut up he'd been over his mother's death, how he felt responsible, how much he understood Sophie's grief. They'd been honest and open. Which was why she'd been so confused when he hadn't called.

He leaned forward and caught her gaze. 'Sophie, I didn't intend for this to happen. I was going to call. I don't usually—'

'Sleep with someone after just meeting them? Me neither. Ever.' She hadn't had so much as a first date with a guy for over two years. 'You were my first and only. Didn't work out like I imagined.'

'And now I have a son.' He looked as if he was struggling to keep a lid on his emotions. He pressed his lips together and they sat in silence for a few moments, both absorbing this life-changing information. He looked bereft and yet animated at the same time. His fingers rubbed his temple, pushed into thick dark hair that was so much like his son's, and those eyes— the exact same blue. Lachie had inherited her nose and mouth, but there was so much of him that belonged to his father. Finn shook his head. 'So what do I do?'

'About…?'

'About Lachie. What do you want? What does he want?'

Where to start? Two parents who were available and around and attentive, unlike the childhood she'd had. 'Lachie's pretty easy to please.

He's a toddler; he wants attention, ice cream and more of those stickers you gave him yesterday. Tomorrow he'll want something else.'

'He likes them? Are they working?' Finn smiled and his face was transformed, and she was spun right back to yesterday when he'd made Lachie laugh. Right back to that night when he'd done so much more than make her laugh. There was something about him that still intrigued her, attracted her, if she was honest. He was still insanely good-looking and, with the cocky edges rubbed off, even charming.

But she couldn't trust him, not with her heart or her son's. She needed to tread carefully. 'He's too young for star charts really, you know. It's probably just novelty value that made him sit still last night.'

'Oh. It works for other kids.' Finn looked as if he'd been stung. 'But you're probably right. What do I know? I only met him yesterday; I have no idea what would work for him.'

'I'm sorry, I didn't mean that the way it came out.'

'You know him, I don't. I have a lot to learn. I don't know where to start.'

He really did look lost and she felt fleetingly sorry for him. He had a lot to take on board. Her son—their son—was a mini hurricane and Finn had no idea about the chaos a child could cause to his life. That was why she was worried about getting him involved with Lachie at all. How could she risk her son's happiness by introducing him to a potentially absent father? Finn hadn't exactly showed 'stickability' or reliability, but he had a right to get to know his boy. She was struggling here between her conscience and her son's needs.

'You learn as you go. I didn't know everything the minute he popped out. It was a huge learning curve that doesn't look like it's going to flatten out any time soon.'

He shook his head. 'So how do you see this working? I have to confess I'm struggling here. Only, if I have a son I will do my best by him. No hesitation.'

'I need to know you're committed to him. That you're not going to randomly bounce in and out of his life and hurt him.'

Shock rippled through his gaze. 'You've got a pretty poor opinion of me. I know we don't know each other very well, but you need to know I wouldn't do that.'

They didn't know each other at all, really. They'd made a baby but all she knew was that he was beautiful and completely unreliable. 'I'm sure you believe you'll be the best of fathers but I'm not willing to take a risk on you spending time with Lachie if you're going to disappear when something else comes along.'

His eyes darkened to navy as anger started to rise again. 'I have a right to get to know him. I'm sure there's a law or something.'

That was the last thing she needed: some kind of injunction to add to being a working single mum and surviving each day. It was in all their interests to work this through smoothly. 'I know. I know you have. But let's just do it slowly.' Then she could assess his impact on Lachie's life and flight risk. 'Baby steps.'

Finn glanced down at his leg and his whole body tensed as if he'd just remembered something. He looked back at her with a bleakness that tugged at her heart and raised so many more questions. 'I don't know if I'm even capable of that.'

CHAPTER THREE

'WHAT HAPPENED?' As Sophie followed the line of his gaze down to his leg, she lost the straightened back and tight jaw and softened into everything he remembered from that long-ago night: concerned, gentle, compassionate. Colour had come back into her cheeks and her eyes were warmer now as she looked back at him. Her head tilted to one side and she smiled. Just enough to make his gut tighten.

It made him want to tell her everything. But he stuck to the medical details; she'd be able to find them easily enough if she looked him up on the health board database. Unethical, but possible, if she felt the need. 'It wasn't just the phone that fell down the mountain. I went with it.'

'Wow. That must have been scary. But you're alive, that's something. Thank goodness.' She looked at his leg again, then at the rest of him and it felt strange to be scrutinised by a woman who'd seen him at his physical best. 'How badly were you hurt?'

He wondered what she was expecting him to answer when he numbered off his injuries. 'A broken pelvis. Cracked spine. Dislocated shoulder. Displaced collarbone. Head injury. Frostbite. Hypothermia…' He waited for all that to sink in, watched her eyes widen. He looked for pity, thought he might have seen it mixed in with her shock. 'And my pièce de résistance…lower left leg amputation.'

'Oh,' she gasped. He searched for revulsion now but didn't see that. 'I'm so sorry—that must have been hard to get over.'

Was an understatement. 'I'm still on that upward climb.' He armoured himself against the inevitable. 'So this is where you leave, right? After all, a useless father is worse than none at all.'

She frowned, taken aback. 'Are you for real? Is that what you think? I've had a useless, absent father myself, which is why I don't want that for my son, and I work with enough broken families to see how much damage half-hearted and selfish parents can wreak on a child's life. I just want him to have a dad, Finn. One leg or two, I don't think he'd care so long as he was around on a regular basis.'

But Finn cared, and because of that he was having second thoughts about getting involved at all. What kind of pride would shine in his son's eyes when his dad lost the fathers' race at sports day or needed a chair to watch him play football because standing too long hurt too damned much? None.

He felt a tight fist of pain in his gut. And how could he protect his son from hurt? He didn't exactly have a good track record on that front. If he'd been a better person, been more reliable and less self-focused, his mother might still be alive and he might have had two legs instead of one.

No. Much better that he took some steps back and didn't get involved. 'Maybe it would be better if I stayed out of the picture. Stay in touch, obviously. I'm invested here, and I'll pay what's necessary and more. I imagine I owe a lot in child support.'

Those caramel eyes burnt hot. 'What? You think this is about money? You think I want anything from you? I've managed by myself and can keep on doing that if you don't care enough to see him.'

He thought about the little kid he'd met yesterday, the grumpiness that he'd clearly inherited from his dad. The sunny smile he'd got from his mum. Something fierce bloomed in Finn's chest. 'I care enough to not see him. I don't want him to be ashamed. That's a lot to live with for a child.'

'For God's sake, Finn, listen to yourself. He needs love. He needs a dad in his life, someone who is emotionally available, but if you're not up to it we'll be just fine without you.' Sophie scraped her chair back and stood. She tugged a piece of paper out of her bag and thrust it at him. 'I've written some details down for you, just in case you lose your phone again. It's all there: date of birth, weight at birth, milestones, medical issues. Likes, dislikes. I thought you might want to know. And he drew you a picture on the back.'

He had his first picture. From his son. *Holy hell.* That gave him a jolt of pride right in the centre of his chest.

Sophie was shaking her head, her ponytail swinging, eyes blazing. So utterly at odds with the woman he'd shared the night with. This was a lioness protecting her young. She was vibrant, strong and determined. This was what parenting did to you and even though he'd only known about his child for a matter of minutes he felt the stirrings of that inside him. 'He drew me a picture?'

'Don't worry; I just said it was for the nice man at the clinic. I didn't mention your real connection, just in case—'

'In case I didn't want to know?' Shame flooded through him; of course he wanted to know. How could he not? How could he deny the boy this right? Deny himself the dreams he'd had growing up? He picked up the paper, which had some of the superhero stickers on it and brown and yellow crayon squiggles. His heart contracted. 'I won't lose it, I promise. Thank you. Please sit down; let's talk this through.'

Her eyebrows rose. 'No. You need time to think and I have to go; it's bedtime and I don't want to wear out my friend's generosity.'

'I imagine things have been difficult for you. To get time for yourself.'

She stiffened. 'I manage.'

He didn't want her to go and told himself it was because he needed to sort all this out today. 'We could both go to your house now and talk, work out a plan.'

She took a step back, palms raised. 'Whoa. No way. A minute ago you wanted to stay away, now you want to see him this minute. Like I said, Finn, we need baby steps and we need to draw up some rules. Have a think about it all and email your expectations through to me. I'll do the same. Then we can talk further. Then, and only then, can you meet him for a supervised visit.'

'Supervised visits? You've pulled out the big words for this.' He knew why. He hadn't exactly proven himself, not just once but repeatedly. He'd wavered from promising he'd be the best father in the world to shying away from the realities of his missing leg and his limitations. But proper unconditional love overrode those things.

She shrugged. 'I don't know you and I'm

damned sure I won't let you hurt my child. I'm just protecting us all.'

If she was intending to rile him it was working. She was clearly very protective of Lachie, and he admired that, admired how she'd brought up a good kid on her own. But her lack of faith in him stung.

'*Our* child, Sophie. I'm his father; I won't hurt him.'

She shook her head and he could tell she was not going to give in easily. 'You provided some DNA, Finn. Let's just see how much of a father you can be.'

'Hi, I'm back! Thanks so much for having him for me.' Sophie bundled through the door of her late grandmother's house and found her friend Hannah sitting on the sofa in front of a blazing coal fire, playing with Lachie and a digital tablet. Her heart squeezed as he looked up and grinned. Her boy. Just hers for a few precious months, really, and now she was having to share him… Was she doing the right thing by letting Finn in?

She didn't really have a choice if she was going

to be able to live with herself, one way or another. Time would tell.

She let all the anger and irritation and the surprising jolt of attraction go—the guy had been through a lot and yet he was still gorgeous, still capable of being serious and yet funny. Still hot enough to make her heart race and her palms itch to touch him. He was all the things she'd promised herself not to get involved with. She needed to be just a mother now. 'How's my boy been?'

'Very good—eaten all his supper and had a nice play.' Hannah wriggled out from Lachie's grip, planted a kiss on his head and grabbed her coat and bag. 'Bye-bye, Lachie! Be good for Mummy.' She leaned close to Sophie and whispered, 'I thought I'd leave the torture device to you. I'm not brave enough to tackle that. I want him to like me.'

'The boots and bars? Hush now. They're for his own good.'

'I know. I just don't like conflict.' Hannah wandered towards the door and waited for Sophie to join her. There was a teasing light in her eyes and Sophie's heart fell. Because, knowing

Hannah, she wouldn't be allowed to get on with the evening without an interrogation. 'How was the dad?'

Gorgeous. Enigmatic. Inspiring. Probably useless.

'Shocked, but I think he'd worked it out. So I'm glad I fronted up and told him.'

'Does he want to be involved?'

Sophie put down her bag and went to stoke the fire, absentmindedly answering her friend. 'With Lachie?'

'Of course with Lachie.' Hannah glanced over to the little boy on the sofa swiping pages and telling himself the story he knew off by heart, and then back to Sophie. 'You didn't think I meant involved with you…' Her eyes grew. 'You don't want…do you? I mean…you did like him once. Enough to sleep with him, and that's not like you at all.'

'Hush! No. Of course I don't want to be involved with him.' She didn't. She really didn't. 'I can't trust him as far as I'd throw him. My heart's not part of the deal, nor my body. I told him Lachie needed a father; I didn't mention anything about a family.' Which was ironic, really, given all she'd ever wanted was a proper family of her own. But she had that now. Her and her boy.

Hannah seemed to have other ideas. 'Still eye candy though?'

'Outwardly, yes, gorgeous. Inwardly, a little hung up. He had an accident and I think it's shaken him up.' But hell, losing a limb would have an effect on…everything. 'You know it's not about how good-looking he is; it's about what he can bring for Lachie. I really wish you'd never got that eye candy information out of me.'

Hannah winked. 'What's a best friend for?'

'Babysitting?'

'Any time. I love that boy. *Ciao bella*. Love you too.' Then she darted out of the door, blowing a kiss. If it hadn't been for her, Sophie would never had stayed sane over the last couple of years.

Closing the door behind her friend, she took a deep breath and tried to get rid of the strange feelings she'd had since seeing Finn. Through two and a half years of silence she'd been downright annoyed, then frustrated, then, to varying degrees, angry all over again. Eventually the simmering anger had faded into…nothing. She'd had no feelings about him at all. Until yesterday, when her ire had risen again, punctuated with the annoying fluster of being with someone who she'd been too honest with.

And then there was the giddy heartbeat and the uplift in her gut just to be around him and the little tug in her belly—stirrings of something she'd forgotten she was even capable of: attraction.

Damn him for appearing just as she was getting her life into some kind of routine after the craziness of childbirth and learning how to be a parent, especially when she'd had little blueprint for that from her own parents. She looked over at the only male she wanted in her life and her heart softened. 'Okay, gorgeous little man, it's time for bed. Come on, let's get that bath run.'

After much splashing and then warm milk he was just about ready for bed. 'Right, let's get on and do your superhero boots.'

'No.' Lachie waddled to the other side of his bedroom and hid in the wardrobe. 'No.'

'Hey…don't forget you'll get the stickers. That nice man, Finn, at the clinic said you could have stickers.' This was always wearing. The fight, the fight, the fight. She crawled over to the wardrobe and opened the door, found him sitting on the floor, his mouth set in an expression she'd seen on Finn earlier. *God, they were similar.* She'd pretended she hadn't noticed before, but it was stark now. She put her hand on his leg and tickled. 'Come out, Mr Monster.'

'No. No boots.' The kid had started to string two words together now and she'd be so proud of him if he hadn't learnt the word 'no'.

'I'll get the stickers and you can have one if you come out. You can have more if you sit still.' She crawled back across the floor, opened a drawer in his cupboard and took out the stickers. Then she put on her sing-song voice. 'One sticker for Lachie. One sticker for Lachie. Oh, this is a good one. Lachie's favourite.'

After five minutes or so of playing this game to herself her boy eventually crawled out of the wardrobe, too nosy to be able to resist. 'Dicker.'

'When you have the boots and bars on.'

He shook his head.

She nodded and held the boots out. 'Let's put them on now. Now, Lachie, or no stickers at all.'

He didn't make eye contact but he sat on the floor and put his feet out. She tugged him onto her lap and showed him the boots with yesterday's stickers stuck on. 'One sticker for one foot and one sticker for the other.'

She didn't want to admit it, but the stickers had been a great idea.

Her mind did a leap from her son's feet to his father's. It was the first time she'd allowed herself to really think about Finn's leg. She'd managed to keep her face straight when he'd told her about the amputation, but she couldn't imagine how terrible that would have been for him. How hard that would have been to get over for a physical guy like him. And then there'd been the rugby…losing a leg would have been an absolute game changer for his sport, and it would have meant he'd have had to redefine himself.

That took guts. A lot of guts. There he was walking, working, giving. Coming up with solutions to help her—and yes, it was only a tiny thing, but it changed the dynamic between her and Lachie; it gave them something fun and rewarding and it worked…and for that she was grateful.

She felt a catch in her throat as Lachie sat still. She wiggled both feet into the boots and then snapped on the bars.

Your dad would be proud.

Whoa!

Where had that come from?

An hour later she was sipping a glass of red wine, staring at a book without seeing the words and trying hard not to think about Finn when her phone beeped.

Hey. This is Finn

Typical, just as she was starting to relax. Her heart tripped and she ignored it. He was not going to get under her skin this time. She was tempted to write *Two and a half years too late* but didn't and instead texted back:

Oh. Wow. This is a first. You didn't lose your phone, then?

Almost immediately he replied:

Ha-ha. No. Never again. Listen, I don't need time to think about this. I'm in. 100%. When can we meet?

It was, if she was honest, a little hurtful that he hadn't texted her after that night but was texting her now she had his son. But at least she knew where she stood; she was the mother of his child and nothing more. Good. That was what they needed. What she needed.

She texted him back:

Rules first.

Again, the reply came almost immediately:

Scary lady. What kind of rules? I won't give him whisky, or let him play with knives, or drive my car.

She laughed to herself. If only it was that simple.

Gah! Where to start? He needs boundaries.

Don't we all?

Judging by the way she was smiling to herself and imagining Finn reclining on that hotel bed, hair all dishevelled...naked...she was the one needing boundaries the most.

He needs lots of love and rewards for good behaviour.

Again, don't we all? Does he get treats for being a good boy?

She laughed.

He's a child, not a puppy.

Oh, aren't they the same thing? Do I scratch his ears and rub his tummy and teach him tricks?

She flicked back at once:

Not if you want to keep me happy.

A message was back in seconds:

Of course I want to keep you happy.

It's because I'm Lachie's mum, nothing else. But hot on its heels another message arrived:

Sophie, I'm sorry about…everything.

Her throat felt suddenly raw. She'd judged him and hadn't known what was happening in his life.

Please stop being so nice. And I'm sorry about your leg.

I have another one, it's okay. ;-)

She knew it wasn't. How could it be? How could he have dealt with losing a limb and the self-esteem issues that came with it and still be funny? But she knew the one thing he didn't need was her pity. She didn't really have any; if anything she was amazed by his resilience. Although she remembered his mental wobble when he'd briefly thought he wasn't fit to be a parent.

And I'm sorry about your collarbone and pelvis and spine and hypothermia and... I can't remember the rest of the injury list.

Just start at the As and work your way through the alphabet, basically.

He'd needed rebuilding, on the outside *and* the inside, probably. No wonder he was gruff at times. He was probably still in physical pain—those kinds of injuries didn't just heal and stop hurting.

I can't imagine how that would have been for you. If I remember, you played rugby or something...?

Ah, yes...my glittering rugby career. You'd never heard of the Swans, right? Top of the Scottish league. I was their best player. And then I wasn't. Stuff happens. So, anyway... Can we meet? If we both have a nine-to-five maybe we could do something at the weekend? The three of us? You can see if I'm suitable.

I know you're suitable.

She had no choice. He was Finn's dad and he'd been through so much she couldn't deny him the chance to get to know his child. If anything it could be healing, give him something other than his broken body to deal with—something positive. And now she was starting to feel sorry for him.

No more messages came through for a while, and she thought the conversation was over until halfway through another glass of wine when she received another one.

It was a good night, Sophie.

She'd lived in Edinburgh ever since that night and had never again stepped inside the pub where they'd met. Had always skirted her path away from the hotel they'd spent the night in. But that hadn't stopped her thinking about it. Thinking about the way he'd kissed her and the need she'd felt for him. She'd never felt so connected to someone, so wanted. And, whatever else he'd done or not done afterwards, she knew he'd felt the same, at least for a few hours. Her body prickled with the memory, a hot rush of need. And, despite everything, they'd produced the love of her life.

She typed on her phone and sent a message back.

It was. A good night…

Then she tapped quickly and sent another message before she had the chance to second-guess herself.

We're going to the butterfly centre on Saturday. Meet us there at two o'clock.

Wouldn't miss it for the world. I'll stick to the rules, don't worry.

She threw the phone onto the cushion next to her and her mind started playing the him-naked-on-the-bed images over and over, and this time she didn't try to stop them.

Truth was, it wasn't him she had to worry about breaking the rules. It was her.

CHAPTER FOUR

FINN DROVE INTO the butterfly centre car park, his heart thudding as he saw Sophie standing at the entrance with Lachie in a navy blue push-chair, waiting. His hands tightened around the steering wheel, but he managed to unglue one to wave to them.

Lying awake in the dark last night, he'd gone over and over how he should act, but none of his imaginings seemed the way Finn Baird would be.

How would he be? He had no idea. How did a father act? What to say? To do? Should he be a little standoffish? Indulgent? Funny? An edu-cator, grabbing every moment to teach his boy about the world? All he knew was that he didn't want to be like his own father—absent. Not if he could help it.

Sophie peered at the car, nodded and raised a hand, her long hair whipping around in the breeze, then she leaned down to speak to the boy. She was wearing skinny blue jeans and a thick pale blue woollen jumper that hid the body Finn remembered. Skin that had been silk under his fingers. Just the right amount of curves. He wondered how being pregnant had changed her and felt a sharp pang of regret that he hadn't seen her heavy with his baby.

There was so much about her and his son he had to learn. For a start, it seemed she was even more of a stickler for punctuality than he was; they had ten minutes until the allotted meet time and he'd planned to be there waiting for them so they didn't have to witness his ungainly exit from his car. *Too bad.*

He parked quickly, bundled himself out as best he could without falling over and walked as fast as his sore leg would allow to get to them. Trying to look normal, act normal while feeling anything but. Spending a day with his boy was giving him more palpitations than debuting for the Swans in front of twenty-two thousand screaming fans.

'Hi. Am I late? Sorry.'

'No. We just needed to get out of the house. He

was getting a bit stir crazy.' She looked as nervous as Finn felt, but smiled and her eyes were warm. 'You were right; having a toddler is like having a puppy: they need regular feeding and watering and lots of fresh air and exercise.'

'And tummy rubs? Don't forget those.' He smiled to himself ruefully. And regretted saying something so lame. This was worse than a first date and even less predictable. Should he kiss her cheek? *No. Oaf.* He stuffed his hands into his pockets.

'Of course—who doesn't like tummy rubs?' She laughed, her eyes shining, her whole face lit up. *Hot damn, she was pretty.* For a fleeting moment he had an image in his head of the three of them laughing together, tangled up on a sofa. A family.

He shut that idea off straight away. He had no right to think like that. He focused on Lachie: the only reason they were here. Last time, he'd paid little attention to the boy's features, but this time he drank in as much as he could. A shock of dark Baird hair that his mum had obviously tried to tame with a brush, and failed. He could have told her there was no point; the hair did what it wanted. Blue eyes the same as the ones Finn looked into every morning as he brushed his teeth. Cute nose, like Sophie's.

On his mum's bedroom chest of drawers there'd been a photo in a silver frame of Finn at this age and Cal a couple of years older. On a beach somewhere, digging to Australia with plastic yellow spades. The toddler in that photo was the spitting image of this one in front of him. If he'd had even the slightest doubt that Lachie was his son, just looking at him was proof enough.

It was incredible. This boy had his DNA. A Baird in everything other than name.

His chest constricted. He took a deep breath and blew it out. What a responsibility. 'Right, let's get going. Should we let him out of the pushchair for a run around?' Then he realised he had no idea what to do with a child. With this child. With any child, really; he just winged it and tried to make them laugh. And he usually did, but this…he had to get the tone right from the beginning. 'I mean, whatever you think.'

'He's still very slow and unsteady so it'll take us a while to get round. But okay, let's wear him out so with a bit of luck he'll manage the nap he's been fighting for the last hour.' She bent to the buggy and unclipped Lachie's straps like an old hand. She picked him up out of the push-chair and held him in her arms. There was a natural ease between mum and son; they didn't have to think about what to do or what to say to each other—they just knew. Not knowing made Finn's heart ache.

Sophie's smile eased the pain a little. 'Hey, Lachie. This is Finn. You remember him? From the clinic; he gave you the stickers.'

'Hi there, Mr Superhero.' Finn looked over and grinned, noting Lachie had his flashing trainers on rather than the boots and bars. He'd be able to run and walk and chase and catch.

He'd be overtaking Finn in all those endeav-ours soon enough, leaving his old man behind in his slipstream. For a moment Finn felt bereft and definitely wished he had both legs.

But then he gave himself a talking-to. Didn't every kid overtake his father at some point? It was the natural way of things. It wasn't just about the physicality; parenthood was so much more.

So much Finn wasn't convinced he could give, or even knew how.

The little boy looked up at Finn with disinterest and tapped Sophie's shoulder. 'Flies. Flies.'

'*Butter*flies.' Sophie's voice deepened. 'Lachie, say hello to Finn.'

Lachie shook his head and tapped her cheek. 'Flies. Flies.'

'Oh. Okay. We'll just skip the introductions.' Finn laughed. So meeting *Dad* wasn't a biggie for the boy.

Sophie's hand was over her mouth as she laughed too but her eyes were apologetic. 'Sorry—he's far more interested in the butterflies than silly old adults.' But then she grew serious. 'It's how they are. Don't feel like it's a reflection of anything at all. He doesn't understand what all this is about. You're just the guy from the clinic. Come walk with us and let him get used to you.'

Time minus three minutes and it hadn't been a rip-roaring success so far. But what had he expected? To be accepted with open arms? He was just some guy. One who needed to earn his son's trust. And he needed to earn Sophie's too.

He still wasn't sure he was doing the right thing being here, but as the weekend had drawn nearer he'd felt lighter and lighter, excited at the prospect of seeing them; Lachie because he was a good kid who was part of Finn now, and Sophie because… He shifted his mind from her smile and her soft body and glittering eyes, the memory of her moans and the taste of her.

Because she'd borne enough of bringing up a child on her own.

He refused to believe he was excited to see her for any other reason. They had rules now, after all. He had his own too.

They wandered through to the large greenhouse, walking very slowly as Lachie stopped to investigate every little flower, butterfly, stick. Finn ached to hold his son's hand, but it was very firmly gripping Sophie's. He watched as they walked and chatted, how she explained things, took her time pointing out the caterpillars and the transformed butterflies.

He watched too, as she absentmindedly tugged her hair into her hands and let the soft weight of the curls fall down her back. Watched the way her mouth had no end of smiles for her son, how her eyes brightened when he laughed, how she seemed so at ease with him. He remembered that night and the way she'd been the same with him and the stark difference in her manner towards him now. Friendly, but not overly. Tolerating because she had to.

When she had a moment to focus back on him he asked her, 'So where are you two living these days?' He had the address—she'd written it on the back of the picture Lachie had drawn—Finn just craved more details so he could imagine them there.

But he saw the ease disappear, replaced with a guarding in the straightening of her mouth, the dulling of her eyes. She was here because she had to be and nothing more.

'In Drumsheugh Gardens. I inherited my grandmother's house and was going to sell it, but then found out I was pregnant. It's perfect for children; there's a park round the corner and a great nursery and school a short walk away. All the things you have to think about with a little one...' She shot him a look that said *Not that you'd know about all this.* 'Suddenly you have to be in the right catchment area for high schools and buying sterilisers and cots. My life has turned out very differently to how I imagined it would.'

And his life had turned out very differently to the trajectory it had been on too. 'What were you going to do, Sophie? After you sold your grandmother's house?'

Her eyes followed a butterfly fluttering from one leaf to another, never still for more than a few seconds. There was something wistful in her look as she watched it flying freely. 'I was going to put the money into a savings account and travel. I had a volunteer job at a charity in India. Then I was going to travel around the world before I settled down. Which was going to be somewhere exotic where I could sip cocktails beachside and dig my feet into warm sand.'

'Scotland's exotic to some people.' He grinned. 'At least, we get a lot of tourists.'

'Cold sand, though. And midges.' She shook her head, her eyes settling on him, the honey-brown of her pupils darkening. 'It's about being somewhere else, Finn. Doesn't matter how much everyone loves this place, I wanted to escape.'

So he'd stolen her dreams too. Every topic he

brought up led them down a path towards her disappointment in him. 'You could still travel. Plenty of people do with a baby in tow.'

'It's not just about the practicalities; it's about time off from work and…well, money. We have a trip to Whitby for a fortnight this year in a caravan, if I'm lucky and work hard and save up. Portugal next year if the stars are aligned and I win the Lottery.' She shrugged. 'It's a slow way to tick my bucket list off, but by the time I'm two hundred and twenty I might have visited all the places in the world I want to see.'

'It's my fault. I should have called, shared the load.'

She came to a halt. 'Yes, you should have. But you didn't so we got on with it. Besides, having you here wouldn't have made a jot of difference. I was pregnant. I was going to get fat and have a baby and have no more seconds to myself, never mind hours or days or years to travel.'

'And you said you had no one else to help.'

She bristled, her chin lifting. 'I have lots of friends, Finn.' But she relented. 'Of course I can't keep asking them to help me out. We do reciprocate, though, as much as I can with a full-time job.'

'And your parents?'

'They're in Dubai. They love their life there and wouldn't give it up easily just to help me out with their grandchild.'

'Why the hell not?' He needed to stop taking this personally, but a rejection of Lachie was personal. He glanced over to make sure he was safe, but also because he couldn't get enough of looking at him. *His child. Wow.* It was surreal. 'He's their grandchild.'

'It's not how they're made. They've spent their lives travelling—maybe that's where I get the bug from. Just thought of that.' She looked a little pensive for a moment. 'I try hard not to be like them, but clearly there's more to personality than nurture. Dad's an engineer. I was born in Africa, spent my toddler years in Hong Kong then boarding school in Kent. Which I hated. They didn't want me getting under their feet in…now, where were they then? Abu Dhabi…yes. Hard to keep up sometimes. But my grandma took me in and basically brought me up.'

'Which was why you were so cut up about her death.'

'She was my mum in every aspect except name. Yes. She was my family.'

Blinking quickly, she started to push the push-chair behind Lachie as he wove his way slowly through the huge subtropical glasshouse. Butter-flies of every colour flitted between the leaves of thick lush plants bordering the walkway. A pond bifurcated the hothouse and the sound of trickling water had Finn looking out for any dan-ger traps for his boy. Shortly they had to cross a small stone bridge with open fencing either side and he kept his eyes trained on Lachie as he wound from one side of the bridge to the other. This parenting thing was all-encompassing.

Finn couldn't help but call out to him, 'Care-ful, Lachie. Walk in the middle. Good lad.'

Sophie grinned. 'He's fine. The gaps in the fence aren't big enough for him to fall through.'

'I don't know how you manage to stay so calm.'

She laughed. 'And I thought it was just the mums who were overprotective.'

'You should know—being a Health Visitor, you must meet a few.'

'Oh, we get all sorts, all walks of life. Scared mums, nervous mums, earth mothers. Some who can't manage at all…poor things.' She wrapped her arms around her body and rubbed her arms.

And he had a sudden urge to wrap his around her too and hold her tight and rewrite the last two years. But he didn't. 'What happens to the ones who can't manage? Are they the ones whose children end up in care?'

'At one end it's just a case of teaching basic parenting skills and giving them help and confidence that they can do it. Timelines and organisation suggestions, that kind of thing. At the other end we sometimes do have to intervene. We go a long way for a long time and give them the benefit of the doubt before we have to do anything serious. We put specific plans in place and work with social services and the police. Neglect and abuse usually stem from deeper issues: addiction, psychological problems…' She shuddered. 'Why are we talking about this?'

'I don't know.' He'd learnt about all this in a module at Physio school, but she was at the coal face. She had an emotionally demanding job and had brought up a good kid on her own. 'I guess not everyone's as capable as you, Sophie. You've done amazingly well. For some people parenting isn't innate or straightforward. Lucky I'm a fast learner.'

She eyed him sideways and smiled, cheeks a pretty deep pink. 'Is this your charm offensive starting again?'

'Me?' He pretended to be affronted. 'I'm all charm and rarely offensive.'

Laughing, she shook her head. 'Could have fooled me.'

'You just need to get to know me.' The conversation about her grandmother had been lost somewhere and he didn't want to bring the sadness back to her eyes by going there again. It was hard to converse openly while distracted by a toddler, but he'd have to get used to it. 'Have your parents ever met Lachie?'

'They made a flying visit when he was about ten weeks old.' She smiled grimly. 'Mum's used to having staff do everything for her so she wasn't exactly a help. *Make me a cup of tea, darling. Gin and tonic, heavy on the gin.*'

'And you did.' He'd had the impression Sophie was strong and independent, but clearly she had issues with boundaries and her parents.

'Oh, I made the first one. She was a guest after all. And the second. Then when she asked for a third I told her to make her own and one for me too. She wasn't impressed. She took photos of Lachie to show off to her friends then went back to her hotel, flew out the next morning. To be honest, it was a relief to have them gone. Less work all round.'

So no problems with boundaries then. Every time he learnt something new about her she went up in his estimation.

Her family life had been so different to his experience. His father had never been around, but his mother had lavished him and his brother with attention. She'd never had much money but made up for that with her time. His heart lurched at the thought of her, that she could well still be alive if it hadn't been for him and his selfishness. He had a lot of making up for his stupid self-absorption when he was younger. Starting here.

'So what can I do to make it up to you? To you both?'

She peered at him, looked at his hands and shook her head. 'No. I can't see a magic wand there.'

'Ach, I'm hiding it. I only bring my wand out for very special people. Play your cards right…' *Geez, what the hell was that supposed to mean? What was he doing?*

Making her laugh and that in itself was magical. Her body lit up and her cheeks reddened. 'Finn Baird, I do not know how to take that.'

Neither did he. 'I'm sorry, I have no idea where that came from.'

'Can't help it, eh?' She looked up at him from under thick dark lashes. Her smile was just outside the friend zone boundary, nudging into flirting, and he was surprised at how that made him feel. How, despite everything, there was a pull to her that he couldn't explain. She tutted. 'You really do know how to spin a line, but don't think I'll be taken in a second time. Not for a minute.'

'Too bad.' He raised his shoulders and smiled, trying not to be over friendly but wanting to be all at the same time. There was something about her, with her lovely smile and bright eyes and soft manner, that tugged at his heart and his gut and, yes, at his resolve. 'But really, Sophie, there's no line. I know where we stand here. Seriously. I just like to make you laugh.'

Her eyes widened and she blinked. 'Well, it has to be better than the way you've been making me feel for the last few years.'

'Blamed for something I didn't even know I was doing.' This time he laughed too. 'So, seriously, how can I make things better?'

'You can't do anything, Finn, except be here for Lachie now and in the future.'

'At least now I understand why you're so adamant he has a father who stays around. Something you didn't have.'

She shook her head. 'I probably shouldn't have told you all of that. They're Lachie's grandparents after all; I don't want to turn him against them.'

He imagined she'd never said a bad word to Lachie about his absent father either; that was the way she was—gentle and undemanding, as if she didn't feel she had a right to complain or ask for things for herself. 'It's okay. I won't say anything about them. Not my business.' He nudged her gently. 'Families, eh. Who'd pick them?'

'Some are okay. Most, actually. What about yours?'

Ah. Yes. 'One meddling brother who I sent off to the other side of the world because he was far too involved in my life.'

Her eyes glittered as she looked at him and laughed again. 'You didn't! You sent him away? How did you manage that?'

'He was all cut up because he thought my accident was his fault. I couldn't get a moment's peace without him interfering in treatment, rehab…what I ate, what I drank. So I concocted a plan to have him go on a course for three months to get him out of my hair. Worked a dream. He's met a woman over there and wants to settle down. Couldn't have worked out better.'

She'd pulled up short and was looking at him, greedy for more information. 'And was it? His fault? How did it happen?'

Not going there. How to say that politely? *Hedge. Talk about something else. Misdirect.* 'Ach—'

'Lachie! Don't touch!' In a flash Sophie had moved towards Lachie, who was reaching out to a hatchling butterfly hanging down from a plant at toddler level. 'He's not exactly gentle.'

Saved by his son. He had a feeling it wouldn't be the last time. Relief flooded through Finn. He didn't want to have to revisit that night, the state he'd been in. Although he knew Sophie would be understanding, she'd try to talk him into believing something different about himself. That he was ultimately good. What did she know? He refocused on the boy: the one truly good thing Finn had ever done.

'He's just interested and doesn't realise how fragile they are.' But Lachie was still reaching perilously close to the butterfly.

Sophie's eyebrows rose. 'But he does need to learn. Lachie, love. Be careful. Good boy. These are just babies. Gentle. Gentle.'

They both reached out to stop him from tearing the delicate wing off, their hands meeting as they touched Lachie's arm at the same time. As his fingers touched Sophie's skin a frisson of something stirred deep in his gut. She laughed softly as she pulled her hand away, clearly not feeling the same weird sensation Finn had. 'Little devil. He needs watching every second.'

Finn caught her gaze and for a beat the laughter died, replaced with something else. The sensual sweep of attraction, the sweet scent of pheromones swimming languidly between them. Suddenly he was back to that night, reliving the raw desire he'd had for her that had sprung from her easy laugh and the depth of the connection they'd shared.

Then Lachie started to grizzle and she turned to their son and breathed out deeply.

Finn's gut started to free fall and he looked away. Nothing good could possibly come of any attraction, particularly on his side. He had a child, but he wasn't about to take on a family. And not a woman like Sophie, who deserved so much more than he could give.

CHAPTER FIVE

SOPHIE PULLED HER hand back from Finn's as quickly as she could, spooked by the tingles shooting over her skin and the stirrings deep in her belly, like something waking up after a long, long sleep. It hadn't just been the touch of his hand, or his citrus and leather scent that sent shivers of memory through her and teased her hormones into life; it had been the easy way she'd been drawn into flirting with him.

She knew what he was like. Knew she had to keep her distance. But knowing wasn't anything like feeling. And she definitely had felt the rush of excitement as she'd talked about his…magic wand.

Charmer. She smiled inwardly. He hadn't lost his appeal. And just for a moment it had been fun to think about something else other than bars and boots and nappies and work.

Trouble was, it had reminded her of what

she'd been missing…or avoiding…for so long. She swallowed, bundled a grumpy Lachie back into his buggy and changed the subject. 'Right, let's go see the snakes. They have feeding time soon and we can get to touch one. And a tarantula too.'

Next to her, Finn shuddered, back to his teasing normal self. 'I did not know you'd brought me to Hell.'

'Scared?'

'Not of spiders.' He feigned nonchalance, but his wide eyes belied him.

'Snakes?'

'No.' He shuddered again, this time with enough drama to make her laugh along.

'You want to say that with a little more certainty?'

'No.' He laughed. 'We are genetically programmed to be scared of snakes and spiders. I'm just reacting exactly as my DNA dictates.'

'Oh, a textbook human?' She played along. 'It's not as if you're out in the wild, man against beast, though, is it? You'll be able to hand him back to the keeper if it gets too much for you. You should face your fears, right?' Just like she was—taking a risk on Finn and some sort of shared parenting future.

But Finn faced his demons every day, she knew. It took a lot of guts to face what he'd lost and come out with a smile for his clients. For her. He shrugged. 'You wouldn't let me live it down if I didn't, right?'

'Not a chance.' She winked and turned to go, all the better to keep a distance from him. From the intoxication of his smile.

They wandered out to a large decked area outside the snake house where a handler was doing a show-and-tell with a huge gold and black python wrapped around his neck. Above them birds squawked in the clear blue sky and there was a reassuring scent of earth and animals. Sophie inhaled and tried to stay grounded as she once again unclipped Lachie from his pushchair and lifted him out so he could see the action. He was groggy and curled his arms around her neck and refused to look at the snake man or Finn. She squeezed her son against her chest and smelt his little boy scent, feeling the weary weight of him in her arms. He laid his head on her shoulder and she felt him give in to the pull of his afternoon nap.

These were the moments she loved—the total trust of a toddler who didn't want to sleep without the comfort of his mum. Hearing the heavy sighs as he fell deeper into slumber, breathing in the sweet smell of him. The feeling of absolute unconditional love in her heart, in her body. These were her moments. Moments, she realised with a sharp pang, she didn't want to share with anyone.

Would things change between her and Lachie now his father wanted to be in their lives? And how long would he be here? Long enough for her and Lachie to fall for him? Long enough to take a piece of their hearts and then what? Once he got to know them would he want to hang around? Or would he do what her parents had done and flit off for his own adventures without her. Or her boy. Would he even turn up when he said he would?

She knew well enough how sitting around waiting for parents to fulfil their promises—and then failing to—made your heart hurt.

So she didn't want to share if it meant shifting

the equilibrium or losing her power. Didn't want anyone driving a wedge between her and the boy who had been her world for so long. Didn't want to stand on the doorstep and watch them head off to have fun without her. To hear about their adventures and not be a part of them, to watch her boy grow under the guidance of a father.

She glanced over to Finn, who was recoiling from the offer to touch the snake and looking at her and laughing…then stopping as he caught sight of her cradling Lachie.

There was something in his eyes that was shaped for her boy. Something she could see swelling and growing as Finn interacted with Lachie.

Sharing was so hard, but she did have to try. She had to at least make an effort, for all their sakes. Because Lachie deserved someone else to look at him the way she did.

'Getting heavy?' Finn's eyes flicked to Lachie's sagging body and then back to her. He looked torn, as if he hungered for something but didn't know how to ask for it. The man was trying. He was here at least, which was more than some men would be when presented with a child. He hadn't run away. He hadn't been difficult.

That was part of the problem, besides the charm and the fun and the gorgeous deep blue eyes that seemed to enchant her all over again— he was a decent man. She dug deep. Tried to share a little of the wonders of being a parent.

'You get used to it and your carrying muscles just grow at the same rate the babies do. But yes, I'm going to have arms like a weight lifter by the time he's four. Do you want to hold him?'

'Won't he wake up?' But Finn's whole face lit up at the offer.

'No. Once he's asleep he's completely out of it.' She looked down at Finn's legs and realised he'd probably need help to do that. *Damn. Inconsiderate.* 'Would it be better if you sat down and I put him on your lap?'

His eyes flashed dark. His jaw clenched. He lifted his chin, snapping back at her, 'I'm not an invalid, Sophie. I can stand up and hold my child.' Fighting. Proving himself. The first time she'd seen that side of him. And she understood. Understood he wouldn't want to be seen or treated as different to anyone else. Even though he was, in so many ways.

She wondered what his leg looked like, what he was like now underneath those clothes. Then pushed that thought away. You didn't judge a person on how they looked, although no doubt Finn was still one hundred per cent Sex God despite his scars.

And she so shouldn't be thinking like that.

'I didn't mean you couldn't manage. I was thinking sitting down would be more comfortable; it usually is. He gets heavy. Now it's my turn to say sorry.' She bit her lip and her hands shook as she handed Lachie over, cradling his head with one hand and wrapping her other arm under his bottom. She watched as Finn mirrored her arms, took all his own weight on his right leg and cradled the boy onto his right shoulder. It looked incongruous but stable. He was a grown man, he knew his limitations; she had to trust him at least about that. She lowered her voice so as not to wake Lachie during the transition. 'I'm just a bit…well, nervous about all this. Not you. This. Playing families.'

As he registered that, Finn's shoulders dropped

and he found a small smile. His head touched his son's crazy curls and Finn's whole body seemed to soften and yet solidify with pride all at the same time. For a moment she had to look away as her heart ached with something she couldn't describe, but she was drawn back by Finn's voice. 'It's all a bit sudden and a bit of a surprise, right?'

At least he understood a bit of what she was going through, though she doubted he'd ever fully know what it was like to feel so abandoned, so alone and then to dig deep and survive. Pouring everything she had into the boy she'd carried in her belly and her heart. And now she was having to let go a little of that symbiosis she had with Lachie, for a man she wasn't sure fully deserved it. 'I'm trying to get used to it. It's just weird, sharing him with someone else. No one else carries him usually... I just needed to be sure... I'll get used to it.' She had no choice now; she'd opened the door and let all these obstacles rush in at her perfectly imperfect life.

Finn nodded. He closed his eyes briefly then opened them and caught her gaze. She liked him when he made her laugh, but God, he was impressive when he was fighting. 'I hadn't thought about it like that. You're giving up a lot for me. I shouldn't have snapped at you. And…don't worry about being gentle around me… I hate fussing—it's what my brother does and it drives me mad…as if he thinks I can't decide what's best for me.' He shrugged the shoulder that wasn't supporting Lachie's head. 'I'm an adult, Sophie. I might not like having been dragged into being one, but there it is. I can drive a car. I can ride a bike. I can even ski…badly. And, yes, everything I do now is slower than I used to do it. But holding my child is a no-brainer. I'll tell you what I can and can't do, okay?'

'Yes. Okay.' She had to let him lead on that, for sure. He wasn't an invalid and he'd hate to be thought of as that. The father-son moment she'd been hoping for, for Lachie's sake, had been damaged by her thoughtlessness. She needed to find something to make things better, so went for humour. It had been the way they'd got together in the first place in that bar. A shared joke that had led to a shared bed and now this shared child. 'I bet you're only holding Lachie so you don't have to hold that snake.'

'You got me.' Finn's irises lightened to the colour of the sky on a rare Edinburgh summer's day. 'Any excuse not to come into contact with that, but feel free to have it wrapped round your shoulder. In fact...' He raised his free hand and got the attention of the snake handler. 'We have a volunteer right here.'

'Finn Baird—I can't believe you just did that.' She flung her fists to her hips and scowled at him.

He grinned as the snake handler brought the coils closer. 'Now we'll see what you're made of.'

She took a deep breath and let the man drape the snake around her shoulders, making sure to act as if she was taking it all in her stride. 'Wow. It's heavy. And warm and dry. I always thought snakes were slimy or something.'

Finn tried to gently jostle Lachie awake, tickling him gently and whispering, 'Hey mate, you're missing the action. Have a look at Mummy.'

But Lachie just sighed and turned his little sticky head away. Finn shrugged. 'Doesn't want to look at a snake. Smart kid. Clearly the boy has my genes.'

'Er… I think you'll find he has my brains,' she volleyed at him, surprising herself at the lightness and the flirting in her voice. '*That's* why he's smart.'

'My sense of humour, though.' Finn laughed. He caught her gaze again and the laughter melted away. His eyes burnt bright with a longing that tugged at her belly, at her reserve.

'He's got your…' She couldn't take her eyes off Finn. Nothing to do with the way he shared genes with Lachie and everything to do the raw sex appeal that hummed around him, curling between them and tugging them closer. The breadth of his shoulders she knew she could cling to and they'd hold her tight until she wanted to let go. The kick up of his top lip when he smiled. The glittering eyes that changed colour depending on his mood. Right now they were dark and rich like luxurious blue velvet flecked with gold. 'Er…sticky-up hair.'

'Poor bugger.' Finn laughed. 'And he's got your looks, Sophie…beautiful…'

He paused, seemed to grapple with what he was going to say next. His hand cupped her cheek and his thumb ran slowly over her bottom lip. A shiver of desire lurched through to her core, swirling deeper and tighter and lower, and she leaned towards him. His face was inches away. She could feel his warm breath on her skin, discerned the hitch in his breathing. She saw the desire in his eyes as he kept right on looking at her. And looking. And she felt the same need deep inside her. Her whole body strained for his touch. Voice low, he said, 'I just wish—'

'Wish what?' Her heart began to hammer hard and she had a sudden urge to reach to him. To tiptoe and press her lips to his, to taste him again. To search out that deep physical and emotional connection they'd had and rekindle it. To kiss him.

God, she wanted to kiss him.

But that couldn't happen, definitely not here, with a child in his arms and a snake looped round her shoulders, in front of strangers. It couldn't happen at all. They both knew that. But that didn't stop the ache.

'Nothing.' He turned away. There was something in his manner that changed, as if the enormity of the situation was finally falling into place for him. Or was it something else? What did he wish?

Was it the same thing she'd been feeling and kept pushing away? The tug of attraction. A wish that things had worked out differently? That things could be better? Good even, between them?

The handler interrupted the moment; he had a huge camera and was pointing it at the three of them. 'What a lovely family. Come on, Dad, give us a smile. What's the matter, Dad? Too close for comfort, right?'

'Yes. A little.' Finn's shoulders were up round his neck and he blinked. Swallowed.

She didn't know whether he meant he was too close to the snake, or if he'd wanted a kiss too. Next to her, Finn's body tensed. And Sophie was pretty sure it had nothing to do with the snake getting ever nearer to him.

In Finn's arms Lachie stirred. For a couple of seconds he rubbed his head back and forth across his father's chest then stopped abruptly. Sensing something different, he looked up at Finn and his features folded.

Uh-oh. Meltdown time. Huge tears filled his

baby-blue eyes and a noise erupted from his throat as if his whole world had ended. Then, wriggling and kicking, he reached his arms towards Sophie. 'Mama. Mama.'

She shook her head and smiled as reassuringly as she could. 'Hey, sweetie. This is Finn, remember? He's nice.'

Finn's eyes grew wider and he swayed from side to side—given the heavy lean on his missing leg it was costing him physically—he fixed his jaw and nodded, ear close to Lachie's. 'Hey, buddy. Hey, it's okay. You were asleep. And now, look, Mummy's wearing a snake.'

'No!' Little fists tightened into balls and Lachie hit them at Finn's chest, frowning and arching his whole body towards his mother, away from his dad. 'No!' he shouted. 'No. Mama.'

The contented smile faded as panic and confusion swirled behind Finn's eyes. He held Lachie away from his chest. Arm's length. The peace Sophie had never imagined could ever happen between them immediately shattered. 'Here. You should take him.'

'I'll take Hector.' The keeper helped unwrap the snake from Sophie's neck, although the heavy weight didn't seem to lift from her shoulders. 'Okay. Okay, little one. Mummy's here.' She didn't want to take him. She wanted Lachie to get used to Finn—she wanted father and son to develop something precious and everlasting but it wouldn't work when Lachie was like this. She took hold of her boy and he nuzzled tight against her neck but she kept her eyes on Finn. He seemed to have folded into himself. 'Hey, don't take it personally. He's always cranky when he wakes up.'

'Okay. Sure.' His voice was haunted as he spoke. 'I should probably go.'

'You don't have to.' She tried to make a joke of things. 'Stay a bit longer; we can go see the tarantulas.'

He didn't bite. 'I think it's for the best.' He stuck his hands deep into his pockets. 'I guess he needs to get used to me.'

'Yes. Yes, he does. We all need to get used to each other. It's been a huge step forward but we can't rush it and suddenly bridge the two-year gap in one afternoon.' They needed space to keep their emotions in check. At least she did.

'Stay for the photo at least. Then, yes, we should all go.'

So he found a smile and posed for the camera, then he watched as she laid Lachie back into the pushchair and clipped him in.

Finn seemed suddenly in a hurry. 'Okay. I have to go.'

'I know. It's okay. It's been a big day. Why don't we—' *Try again next week?*

But he wasn't listening and before she could finish he'd turned tail and was heading for the exit. Taking all the good vibes with him and leaving her heart aching, not just for how things had turned out but for the feel of his skin on hers again.

For one kiss.

CHAPTER SIX

BACK AT HOME, Finn collapsed onto the sofa, removed his prosthetic and rolled off the silicone liner. He breathed deeply as the cool air bathed the irritated and red skin. *Freedom. Relief.*

Too much activity and not enough rest. He had to remember to give himself a break.

And yet… If only… So many if-onlys. Too many.

He forced himself to look at it, at the lumpy skin, the still pink stitch marks. The space where a calf and a shin and a foot should have been.

Forced himself all over again to accept it. This was who he was now. No point in wishing otherwise. Although he did. Every day. *God*, how he wished things were different. Not for the way he looked—he was coming to accept that too; there were thousands of people like him around the world, many more who were much worse off— but for the things he couldn't do. He couldn't hold his son without Sophie thinking he needed supervision. He couldn't be seen as capable. At least, not by Sophie.

More, it was a frank reminder of who he was and the stupid, self-centred, immature mistakes he'd made that had, literally, cost his mother's life. If he could barely be trusted to hold his child securely, he most certainly shouldn't be trusted to keep him safe and well. Protect him. Protect Sophie, which seemed to be an innate need, deep in his DNA.

He traced his fingers over the joining fold, the place where they'd taken the smashed and frost-bitten lower leg away and meshed together his skin. Massaged gently until some of the friction pain was rubbed away.

If only he could rub other kinds of pain away too.

His kid didn't like him. Sophie was trying hard to make it happen, but it wasn't the sort of thing that could be forced. His kid didn't like him.

And Finn really liked Sophie—in good ways and over-the-line ways and there wasn't a thing he could do about it.

The heavy beat of a rock song interrupted his

thoughts. Cal. He had a dedicated ringtone so Finn could choose, or not, to answer without having to limp around trying to find his phone. It was the middle of the night in New Zealand but Cal was working the paramedic night shift. Which meant he could ring in the quiet moments. As he did, all too regularly, to check up on his brother's progress.

He hesitated to pick up, but then relented; because he'd only call later and again and again until Finn answered. He flicked the screen and his brother's ugly mug appeared in front of the white sterilised walls of the ambulance station. His phone was propped up on a table and the angle caught his brother's jaw and face close and his voice was loud in the stillness of the Southern Hemisphere night.

'Hey Cal, how's things?'

'Good time? Bad time?' Cal scratched his chin and sat back in his chair, settling in for a long talk.

Uh-oh. 'I've just got in. And I've got a ton of stuff to do.'

'Oh? Tell me more. Where've you been?' The thing about Cal was that he tried hard to be relaxed around Finn but sometimes it was too hard. And it was the trying that got to Finn the most. 'A date? The game? Where?'

'I haven't been to a game of rugby since the accident and I don't think I ever will.'

Cal's eyebrows rose. 'It might be good therapy for you. Facing your demons and all that.'

Geez, everyone seemed to want him to do that these days. 'I don't need to go out of the house to do that; all I have to do is look down at my feet. Foot. And please stop telling me what might be good for me.'

Cal shrugged and slumped back into his chair. Tiredness drew dark circles under his eyes. 'I'm sorry.'

'You look terrible.'

'Trying to fit my sleeping schedule in with the baby's naps isn't exactly working.' He rubbed his face and yawned. 'But, anyway, you should try the rugby...or dating or something. You need a focus.'

Well, boy, did he have one now. 'I know it's because you care, but we've been over this. I'm a grown-up now; I make my own decisions about

what I do.' Which meant he had to take responsibility.

So he should probably tell big brother about
Lachie.

Finn took a deep breath and tried to work out
exactly what to say, how to say it. No doubt
feeling similar to the way Cal had felt only
six months ago when he'd fallen in love with a
woman who was having another man's baby via
surrogacy. Now, that had been confusing, but
there they were, all those miles away, happily
settled. And if he was going to be a good dad
he needed to find someone he could get advice
from. The only man he knew who was a father
was his brother, Cal. 'Listen, I have something
to tell you. Something big.'

Cal immediately frowned, jerking forward, on
alert. 'What? Is it trouble?'

'I don't know.' Because that was the truth of it.

'You okay? Still taking your meds? Because
depression can hit you any time out of the blue.'

'Stop fussing, Cal. I'm fine… I'm over that
now. I know what I have to do, what signs to
watch for. I was down because I lost my leg…
anyone would be, right? But I'm over it now.'

And finding out about Lachie and Sophie had his heart leaping, not sinking. At first anyway. Now he had to get over a zillion hurdles to make it all work. And he had to own this. 'Okay.' He swallowed. It wasn't every day you made this kind of announcement. 'I've just found out I have a child.'

'What? Are you for real? A child?' Cal's head tipped back and he laughed. 'Copycat. You always did the sibling rivalry thing well. I get a child so you get one.' Then he got serious. 'Is it a good thing?'

Was it? Finn had had sleepless nights going over and over what to do, how to be. How things would pan out. 'Yeah. It's good. He's good. He's eighteen months old and he's called Lachlan. Lachie.'

'Wow, Finn. This is a lot to take in. A lot for you to deal with. Are you sure you're okay? You need me to come over?'

'Geez, man. I'm fine. Stay there with your own family. I just wanted to let you know. You're an uncle.'

His brother's eyes widened. 'So I am. Uncle Callum—who'd have thought? Wow, no babies for years then two come along at once. I hope the poor little mite's got his mother's looks and not yours.' His eyes narrowed. Not a good sign—he was homing in, scrutinising. It was his OP as the big brother who'd saved little brother's life. 'Who is she, the mother?'

'Sophie. She's…' This was where things got murky for Finn. He'd never been one to believe in all that love-at-first-sight stuff, but it had definitely been attraction at first sight, and then things had got complicated.

Cal filled the silence. 'One of your famous conquests?'

'No, she was not.' So he'd had a reputation of loving and leaving. He'd been young and immature. But a lot had happened between then and now… In fact, Sophie was the last woman he'd slept with. He didn't know whether to feel sad or proud about that. Proud, actually. 'It wasn't like that. Not at all.'

'Finn Baird, you used to be like that. You had women lining up. You probably still do, knowing you. So what's so special about this one?'

'I didn't say she was special.' But she was and

he'd wanted to kiss her in the butterfly garden. He wanted to kiss her now too.

But then, he'd wanted to kiss a lot of women in the past. Had kissed them. But Sophie? He had a feeling kissing her would mean a lot more than he wanted it to.

Cal was watching him, eyebrows furrowed, but with a wry smile. 'You don't have to say anything, mate. It's written all over your face. Well, this is interesting. She's a keeper?'

He couldn't keep anyone. Didn't Cal know that? 'Tell me, why did I bother picking up when you called?'

'Because you love me.'

He did. He owed him a lot too, if he was honest. But if Cal could step a little back sometimes that would be awesome too. 'You're no help, man. I'm not looking for a keeper or anything else. I just wanted to ask—how do you be a dad? A good one? What do you do?'

Cal settled back in the chair and grinned. 'I'm no expert. Far from it, Grace is only six months old. But I'd say you just do what feels right.'

Kissing his son's mother felt right. Holding her. Making love to her. And he couldn't do that, any of it. Not if he wanted to make things right for his son. 'He doesn't like me.'

'Ach, how could he not love such a bright, bubbly guy like you, Finn?'

'Quit the sarcasm. I mean it. You should have seen him trying to get back to his mum when he woke up and found himself in my arms. He almost screamed the place down.'

Cal's face softened. He quit the jokes. 'You've got it bad.'

'Aye. I think I have.' The fierce helplessness when Lachie had squirmed away from Finn still hung around in his gut. And he wanted to erase it with his kid's giggles. Giggles Lachie only seemed to have for his mum.

Sophie. At just the thought of her his whole body prickled with heat. Even though he'd only seen her twice since the clinic and both times had been blurred with revelations and relearning, and nothing she'd said or done had given any cause for hope that she might want him in any other way than being a father to their child.

He was going crazy. This wasn't some youthful lust thing going on—it was more than that.

Cal was still stuck on Lachie. 'You want to be

part of his life? Hands-on? Not like our dead-beat father?'

'I do.' *More than anything.*

'Then do it. Be there. Make sure you're around. Stickability wins out. Wear him down, mate. Win him over.'

He made it sound so easy, but then he hadn't seen the panic and fear and pure upset in Lachie's face when he realised he wasn't nestled in his mother's arms but in some almost stranger's.

'What about Sophie?'

'That's her name? Right. Win Sophie over too, with the wit, charm and good looks you got from your brother.'

'That's the highest mountain I'll ever have to climb.'

Finn didn't trust himself, so he couldn't expect her to trust him. And now the most important question of all. Not for the first time, he opened his fears up to his brother.

'Cal, what if I can't do it?'

His brother didn't need to read between the lines. He'd been there when Finn had fallen into thin air, had kept him alive through that dark, icy night, had been there—sometimes supremely annoyingly—for every step of Finn's recovery.

What if I can't do it? What if I don't have the guts to follow through? What if I choose the easy route again and cause more damage?

'Listen to yourself, Finn. You were the highest scoring scrum half for the Swans and nothing spooked you. Not the endless taunts from the other teams. Not the crappy refs. Not the stupid commentators. Not the prick of a coach who dropped you. You held your head high and pushed back. You fought tooth and nail to get upright after the accident. You went skiing against everyone's advice. I'm not saying it's going to be easy. But you'll do it, Finn. Because you can't not. Because having that boy and his mother in your life is far, far better than the alternative.'

For once his brother was right; having them in his life would be so much better than knowing they were out there somewhere and that he was missing everything. First day at school. First wobbly tooth. Teaching his boy how to ride a bicycle.

How had their own father managed to cut himself off from his own boys? *God*, Finn had only known Lachie a week and he couldn't wait to see him again.

He made his excuses and said goodbye to his

brother, then flicked to the last message trail he'd had with Sophie. Was it too soon to contact her again?

He didn't care.

How's Lachie?

What he really meant was, *How are you both?* But he didn't want to freak Sophie out by coming on too strong or being too personal with her, crossing a line that couldn't be uncrossed.

His heart hammered as his phone lit up.

Tucked up in bed and asleep, which is where I will be very soon. Big day. Long week.

He thought back to Monday, when he'd been oblivious to the existence of his son. Or of her being so close by. He flicked her an answer, deliberating over every single word. Not too pushy. Not too flippant.

Huge week. Thanks for today. Sorry I bailed so quickly.

His phone lit up again.

It's okay. I understand. We need to take things slowly, introduce you gradually.

He didn't have the patience for all that—he had a lot of time to make up.

How about one evening this week?

Immediately he regretted that. Too pushy. She wouldn't want to see him again so soon especially after he'd almost kissed her. Had she noticed or been too distracted by the snake? Had she felt the same tug of attraction?

But his phone chimed with her reply.

There's a thing at Nursery on Wednesday. A sort of family bring-your-own-dinner open evening with wine. I'll sort the food. You bring wine. White, preferably. Meet me at my work. Six o'clock. We can walk from there. It's not far.

That was quickly followed up…

I didn't mean anything by that last bit…

He smiled. At some point everyone in his life would stop overcompensating for his lack of leg…but not yet, it would appear.

I know. It's okay. Stop overthinking. I ran a five-mile race last weekend. I can walk around the corner. You don't have to tread on eggshells. I don't hop on them... See, I can even joke about it.

I like a man with a sense of humour!

He imagined the sweet turn-up of her lips as she smiled, the gentle sound of her laughter, and he sent her his immediate response:

I like you.

Damn. Why had he said that? They'd been getting along just fine.

There were a few minutes' silence and he figured he'd blown it. But then...

Going to bed now.

He imagined her dark curls on a white linen pillowcase. The soft noises she'd make as she slept. Her scent of apples and vanilla and something flowery in the air. He flicked her another message:

Sweet dreams.

A quick reply came back.

Oh, I'm sure they will be.

Interesting...

About...?

That's my secret...

His heart picked up. His skin prickled. His gut tightened.

Sophie, tell me more...

Finn...

He grinned. This was just being friendly. And funny.

Should I guess...?

Not a good idea. See you on Wednesday. Goodnight.

Slumping back against the sofa cushions, he grinned. He was going to see her again, and very soon. It would be a very good night indeed.

CHAPTER SEVEN

WAITING FOR WEDNESDAY was giving Sophie heartburn.

There was something about Finn she couldn't resist. Couldn't help being playful around him. Couldn't help reacting to his charm with some flirting of her own. And she wondered whether the silly texts had given him the wrong impression.

Or the right one.

He was due at the clinic in twenty minutes and she could barely concentrate on her job.

Which was wrong for so many reasons. Because for this to work between them all there had to be no emotional ties between her and Finn.

Tonight was going to be an introduction to Lachie's nursery and routine, that was all. Nothing more. So there was no point being all silly and giddy. All she had to do was write up her notes, put on some lipstick, grab the food she'd prepared and she could go.

A sharp rap on her office door made her jump. It was Evelyn, the clinic receptionist, her face set in a grim line. 'Jackie Campbell's in Reception with her kids. She said she needs help.'

'It's late. She knows our hours... We closed thirty minutes ago.' Sophie's heart rate kicked up and she scolded herself. Jackie was trying to pull her family up from a life of poverty; she was a good woman who'd had a lot of knock-backs and a tough ride in life so far. Sophie felt inherently sorry for her and her three children. Given they were all under the age of five, they were all her concern. 'What kind of help does she need? What's wrong?'

Evelyn shrugged and shook her head. 'She wouldn't say but she looks rough. And scared.'

It was wrong of her, she knew, but Sophie glanced at the clock and her heart sank. Fitting an unexpected client in now would make her late.

What would Finn do?

Now, that was a thought she'd never expected to have.

He would move Heaven and Earth to help someone in need. He'd already done it for her, so he'd understand if she was running a little late. 'Tell her I'll be out in a minute. I'll just finish up here. Can you grab the kids something to eat and a drink if they need it?'

She heard them before she saw them. But it wasn't just Jackie and her three children; it was Billy now too. A hard man with a history of addiction, he was swaying and not quite focused as he shouted at his wife, 'Get yourself back home and bring them all with you.'

'No. This is the last straw, Billy. You said you wouldn't go drinking again and look at you. You're a mess and you're scaring the kids.' Jackie stood and faced him, pushing her youngest, Billy Junior, behind her thin pale legs. It was May in Edinburgh and in no way warm, but she wore only a thin, creased T-shirt and a short denim skirt that had seen better days. The two other children were in the toy corner playing quietly but glancing over at the action. The saddest part was that they seemed to be used to this kind of scenario.

Sophie took a deep breath and walked towards

them, remembering her negotiation skills training and trying to appear neutral. 'Hey there.'

Jackie whipped round, her shoulders sagging the moment she saw Sophie. She had dark shadows round her eyes and her skin was sallow, cheeks hollow. 'Sophie. Thank God. Can you do something about him? I've had enough. Can you sort out a restraining order or something? I don't want him near us when he's drunk.'

'Don't be stupid, Jax. You don't mean that.' Billy swayed forward onto the toes of his ragged black canvas shoes and then back again, face contorted into a grimace. He was similarly dressed in unsuitable unseasonal clothes, covered only in a T-shirt and jeans. At least the children were all wrapped up warmly, Sophie noted. Jackie always put the kids first even if it meant she went without things for herself.

Sophie found what she hoped was a non-judgemental smile and remained as calm as she could be. This was going to take longer than she'd thought and would require delicate handling. 'We can talk things through, sure.' She turned and faced the wiry man. 'We just need to make sure everyone's safe, Billy, and that we all know the score. You know that. You know how it works. Yes?'

'You! You keep away from my kids,' he snarled, nostrils flared. 'Keep away from my wife.'

Sophie's heart kicked into overdrive. All well and good looking calm and in control on the outside, but inside she was shaking. 'She came to me, Billy. She wants some help and I'll give it to her. I can help you too if you want.'

'I don't need your help. You can't keep me away from my kids. I love them.'

'I know you do, Billy.' Today he looked rough and on edge but she'd seen him on good days, on his hands and knees giving the children rides on his back. Seen him besotted with love and in tears after the birth of each child. Heard him apologise over and over for the way he seemed to lose grasp of his self-control. Like right now when he had anger in his eyes and tension thrumming through his body.

Sophie raised her hands just a little and indicated she was on his side. On everyone's side. Glancing briefly over to Evelyn, she nodded so minutely no one else would have noticed. But

Evelyn nodded back and activated the silent alarm system. Just a precaution. 'We just want to make sure the kids are okay. And Jackie too. You want that, right? You love them and you want them to feel safe.'

'You even think about taking them anywhere but my house and I'll kill you. You got that?' Billy took a step towards her. Then another until he was an inch away from her face. He smelt of booze, fresh and stale. And unwashed clothes. And sweat. Cords of veins stood out in his neck as he pointed a very shaky finger right into her face. Sophie stood her ground, determined not to be intimidated even though her hands were shaking as much as his were and her breathing was far too fast. If she jumped now or moved too quickly he could curl that hand into a fist. He was wiry but he was strong.

She breathed out slowly. 'Billy—'

'Get your hands away from Sophie. Now.'

Finn. Great. Let's add another alpha into the mix.

She fought against her raging heartbeat. *Stay calm.* Keeping all senses alert to Billy and any sudden movements he might make, she half turned to Finn, pushing her palm downwards over and over, indicating him to back the hell off. 'It's okay, Finn. We're working this out, aren't we, Billy?'

Any other day Sophie would have appreciated how damned magnificent Finn looked with his eyes blazing and his muscles primed. She'd even have noticed the way part of her yearned for those taut arms to hold her, the way her heart kicked up just seeing him. Never mind the soft blow to her solar plexus that he was here, protecting her, no matter how misguided she thought him to be.

But right now she was so damned angry that he'd barged in as if she was helpless, she only noticed the prickle of white-hot anger in her gut. *How dare he try to take over?*

One look at Finn, chest all puffed up, jaw set and with his rugby physique making him twice the size of Billy, the drunk man took two steps back. Three. 'I didn't… I wasn't going to…'

'No, you weren't going to, pal. Sit down.' Oblivious to her irritation—or just plain ignoring it—Finn stepped across the room towards the man and stood close until Billy sat down in one of the plastic chairs. 'Has anyone called the police?'

Evelyn raised her hand from behind the desk where she was now feeding the little ones some sandwiches and distracting them by pointing to things out of the window. 'They're on their way.'

'No.' Billy's face creased up. 'They'll lock me up for being drunk and disorderly.'

'Again. You might as well move into Edinburgh jail.' Jackie sat down next to her husband and took his hand. 'Why, Billy? Why do you have to do this?'

'Can't help it.' Billy shrugged and slumped further in the chair, head in his hands as huge tears slipped down his cheeks and onto the linoleum floor, the aggressive drunk phase moving into the morose drunk stage.

Jackie seemed unmoved by the tearful display. 'Benefit day and you have to waste it all on booze. We've been waiting on that money for days. What about the kids? Food? You promised me. *This* time it was going to be different.'

He looked down at his dirty shoes and shook his head. 'Sorry, love. I couldn't help it. I just couldn't. But I won't do it again.'

Sophie's heart went out to them both. She'd followed the family after the births of each of the children. Times were hard for them, but getting him back on track was going to need work. So many times he'd promised to get help and he'd never even made the first step. 'Look, we can get you some food for over the weekend. The food bank's still open. If you come back and see me on Monday morning we can take things from there. Okay?'

Jackie looked up, wiping a hand across her tear-stained face, and smiled wearily. 'Thanks, Sophie.'

'And we need to work out how to help you, Billy.' Finn sat down on the seat the other side of the man. Finn's bravado had been replaced by something akin to conciliation. Understanding. Although he definitely still held the authority. 'Life sucks sometimes, eh? You feel like you're sinking and you can't find a way out.'

'Yeah.' Billy shrugged and ran a hand over his jaw. 'Tell me about it.'

Finn's fingers went to his own chin and he rubbed too. 'You feel like you have to be the man and it's hard. Everyone looking at you for answers and sometimes you just don't have them, right?'

'I can't get a job. I can't pay my way. I can't look after my kids. I was just walking past the boozer and I saw a sign for a barman's job. Popped in to ask about it. But then I couldn't stop myself having a pint. Then another...'

'And then you feel even worse. It's a spiral.' Finn kept his eyes ahead, not looking at Billy, and nodded. Sophie wondered whether he'd had negotiation training too. *Don't hold intense eye contact because it unnerves the aggressive client. Listen. Empathise. Mirror movements to gain trust.* Either that or he was just an innate listener. 'You don't have to carry all this, you know. You can get help. There are people, places who can help and you know what? It takes a big man to realise he needs help. An even bigger one to go get it.'

Billy turned to look at Finn, eyebrows raised. 'Have you...you know...?'

Finn sat forward, elbows on his knees, hands clasped and kept looking forward. 'There was a time. Things got pretty bad. Not drinking, but I felt as bad as you do now. Worse.'

Sophie's chest constricted as she wondered how dark things had got for Finn. How he'd managed to fight his way back to the man he was now.

Billy flicked a glance at Finn's expensive-looking leather jacket and huffed. 'Dinna look like you had it bad.'

Now Finn turned to catch Billy's eye. 'Lucky for me, someone helped. You want help, Billy? Before you lose your family completely? Your wife? Those lovely kids. They need their dad. They need you. But you've got to be in a better state. They deserve that. You want help, just say the word. But you've got to mean it.'

'Nah.' Billy rubbed his trembling hands down his thighs. 'I can manage this.'

Finn nodded. 'Like you did this afternoon?'

'That was different. Just a slip-up.'

Finn nodded again. No judgement, no opinion. 'You have them a lot?'

'Yes, he does.' Jackie looked defeated. 'And I'm sick of pointless promises. I've had enough. This is it. I'm finished with it all. He can go to hell for all I care. In fact, I'd prefer it if he did, then we could get on with our lives without him messing them up.'

Finn shook his head. 'This is a big deal, Billy. I'd say by the looks of her she really means it. Is it worth losing your family—everything—for?'

The man sat for a moment, looking at Finn, then he turned away and looked at his hands. The floor. His wife. The kids. And he nodded slowly, cheeks more hollow, eyes more desperate, saying what Sophie had heard him say so often but never with such determination and meaning. 'Help me, man. Now, though, before I do more damage. Can you sort it?'

'I will. Stay here.' With that, Finn stood and went outside. Made some calls. A siren alerted them to the police arriving, but Finn headed them off.

Sophie watched the faces of the family as relief filled the room. No restraining order. No broken hearts. No broken family—at least no more broken than it was already. When he headed back in, Finn walked straight to Billy and took him back outside. A taxi arrived and took Billy away.

Jackie watched him leave and breathed out slowly. She'd get a reprieve at least and Sophie could work on more strategies to deal with Billy when he came back. 'Thank you. I love him to bits but he drives me insane.'

'Come on, Jackie… I'll give you a lift to the food bank and then we can get those bairns to bed.' Evelyn bundled them all out with a cheery wave and an appointment reservation for first thing on Monday morning.

Which left Sophie and Finn alone with a whole lot of displaced and confusing emotion. Because, no matter what he'd been through, he'd still barged in and tried to take over and he needed to know there had to be boundaries in both their personal and professional lives.

He wandered back into the clinic as if he was meant to be here. 'Right. That's that sorted. Are we going to the nursery now?'

'No, we are not. Not yet.' She willed herself to calm down. After all, this was supposed to be a unifying night, not a breakup one. But she couldn't contain her irritation. 'Who do you think you are, Finn? You can't come charging in like the damned cavalry and rescue me like that. Especially when I don't need rescuing.'

His eyes widened. 'He threatened you, Sophie.

You don't expect me to stand by and watch that happen? Do you? Really?'

No. Yes. No. She was annoyed that he had, but also flattered and impressed he'd felt strongly enough to act. 'I was sorting it out, Finn. He would have calmed down, if you'd given me the chance to talk to him.'

Finn raised his palms. 'Okay, I may have over-reacted. But he just about had his hands on you. I thought he was going to hurt you.'

'I have a panic button which Evelyn pressed the moment we sensed things turning sour—we managed that by eye contact and prior agreement and it's part of our clinic policy. Obviously, I had Evelyn there too—we're never alone if we can help it. I also have a telephone in easy access and I've had a lot of training in dealing with these kinds of things. This is my job, Finn. I know what I'm doing.'

Finn shook his head, eyes adamant and assertive. 'He was two inches away from your face. I'm not going to watch someone I care about being threatened. Never.'

'He's drunk and scared and angry with himself more than anything else. Not me.'

Someone I care about. Something shifted in Sophie's chest and the space filled with a warm glow. But she wasn't going to let it affect her job. She just needed to work on keeping the glow alive in non-work environments. She went over to the play corner and started tidying the toys back into the huge red plastic box.

Finn watched her, came over and sat down heavily on a chair, started handing her some of the displaced toys scattered around his feet. 'Now he's got a place at the Rose Clinic he'll get the help he needs.'

She stopped tidying. The man was crazy. 'The *Rose* Clinic? That's a private place. He can't afford that.'

But he smiled. 'They have a couple of spots they do pro bono. I know the guy who runs it. He owes me a favour.'

Now the crash started to hit on the heels of the adrenaline rush. She started to feel just a little shaky so she sat down next to him and wrapped her arms across her chest. Finn had done a good thing. Maybe she was the one overreacting and being all independent to prove a point. 'Thank you. You did well. I shouldn't be angry. He'll get the help he needs there. Hopefully.'

'I can't imagine how he must feel with the threat of having his children taken away.' Finn frowned. 'I'd… I'd feel like killing someone too.'

He sounded beaten up, taking this very personally. 'Wow. This has really affected you, hasn't it?'

'Of course it has. The whole scenario is nuts. He's got a beautiful family and he's messing it up. If he doesn't sort himself out they'll live with the fallout for the rest of their lives.'

She knew enough about Finn to realise he wasn't just talking about Billy, but about his own father too. He was also talking about himself. Realising what he needed to do as a dad—and yes, it was overwhelming and intense but also incredibly satisfying and beautiful to watch a child grow into a man and he wanted that chance.

She looked over at him and realised her impression of him was changing. He wasn't the charmer so much now—although that was still a part of him that appealed—he was much more than that. Deeper, complicated, damaged—better somehow. Time had changed him, although she guessed his experiences had been the bigger factor. Every day she'd looked at her son and tried to ignore the parts that were Finn, but she couldn't ignore them any more. Didn't want to.

She ached to touch him. But she knew that would take them down a route she shouldn't go. 'What did you mean when you said you'd had dark times?'

A shoulder lifted. 'It's nothing. Just stuff I had to deal with.'

Without thinking, she put her hand on his left thigh. 'Your leg?'

'Er… Yes.' She thought he might reject her touch but he put his hand over hers and squeezed gently before lifting their hands from his leg. 'Boring stuff. I'm over it now.'

'Er… Liar. I imagine all those surgeries and all that healing took its toll. But I'll let it go because you clearly don't want to tell me.'

'Really, no.' He shook his head. 'Why ruin what's going to be a nice evening?'

He was still holding her hand and she was still gripping his and her heart was tripping crazily and her focus seemed fixated on him. Just him and the sensation of skin against skin. His warmth. His scent.

She wanted to know everything about him and she resolved she'd ask him about his dark times again some other time when he wasn't all about showing how good he could be. Developing relationships was about sharing the bad things too.

But they needed more time. Things were happening very fast here and she wasn't sure her head could keep up, never mind her heart. 'Okay, well, don't think you can keep waving your magic wand and solving all my clients' problems.'

His eyebrows rose and he smiled. 'Sophie Harding, you really do seem a little obsessed with my magic wand.'

'I am not.' Okay, she might be a little intrigued. After all, she'd experienced him before and knew what would be in store.

Lust crackled through her at the memory and she should have pulled her hand away from his but she didn't. She should have leaned away from him too, but she stayed exactly where she was, breathing in his scent and enjoying the tingles prickling through her body as he ran soft circles on the back of her hand with his thumb.

He shifted in his seat so he was facing her, lacing his fingers with hers. 'You keep talking about it.'

She laughed. 'I do not.'

'I've met up with you twice and my magic wand has come up both times.' He jiggled his eyebrows up and down and she laughed even more. 'Excuse the pun... But at least I made you laugh and now you're not angry with me any more.'

'Who says I'm not?' She was still a little bit angry but also turned-on and laughing. The whole gamut of emotions wrapped up in response to one package: Finn Baird. She couldn't take her eyes from his face.

Something, the Arctic breeze coming off the Highlands probably, had blown his hair a little awry and she ached to put her fingers just... there...and straighten it. Even though she knew a Baird's hair never did anything it was told to do. She had a feeling it wasn't just their hair that was stubborn and belligerent and just a little wilful.

His eyes sparked a deep intense blue and his

mouth—oh, that mouth—was close enough for her to lean in just a little and press her lips against. Need scuttled down her spine, tightened her limbs, made her insides warm and molten.

What would he do if she just kissed him?

But he tilted his head to one side and the distance between them grew and the moment, the opportunity, was lost. 'Is your job always as intense as this?'

Thank God he'd taken things back a step. She breathed out more heavily than she'd intended but didn't have the resolve to slip her hand out of his. In fact, she wanted to touch more of him. It was crazy. She was crazy. Because there was nowhere they could go with this, too many reasons.

But she didn't let go of his hand. 'It's a mixed bag, which is why I love it so much. It's very rewarding. I see a lot of lovely babies and gorgeous children and I see parents across the spectrum, from families in desperate need to families who are coping just fine, and all of them just want the best for their kids in the end. Some days are lovely, some are intense, some are difficult.'

He gave her a soft smile which reached down to her belly and tugged. 'Today was difficult.'

'Yes.' She finally found enough willpower and slipped her hand from his, stood and picked up her bag. 'And it's not finished yet. We should go.'

'Not yet.' He caught her arm and tugged her to sit back down and she did, so close. Too close. 'Sophie—'

'Finn.' She put her hand between them, onto his chest—to push him away and, yet, to touch him too. To feel his heart beating fast and sure and hard. And for a second neither of them moved. Their eyes locked and she knew that they were on one single trajectory unless one of them was brave enough and strong enough to pull away.

But she knew it wouldn't be her, because she'd just used up the last of her willpower and this was a chance she might never get again.

He reached a hand to the nape of her neck, this time tilting his head towards her. 'Tell me to stop and I will.'

'Don't.' She shook her head.

The pressure of his fingers lightened and he inhaled sharply. 'Don't?'

'Don't stop.' Unable to resist any longer, she breached the distance between them and pressed her mouth on his. Gentle at first, slow and searching, relishing the feel of him, committing him to memory. Because the first time they'd kissed she'd believed they were at the beginning of something. So she hadn't known how important it was to remember the feel and the taste of him. This time, she knew, could be the last. Should be.

Don't stop.

He opened his mouth and she melted against him, climbing onto his lap and wrapping her hands around his neck. He tasted so fine: something fresh, something male, something intense and beautiful. One of his hands still clutched the back of her neck while the other cupped her face, fingers spanning her cheek. Claiming her as his.

And God, yes, she wanted to be, all over again. Even though he overstepped and overreached. Even though he'd disappeared out of her life. Even though…he kissed like a demon. Like a god.

She pressed closer as he slid his tongue into her mouth. Heard a guttural moan escape her throat. Melted at the smooth stroke of his hand down her arm and the smooth slide of his tongue against hers. She pressed closer still, desire spurring her on. She wanted him. Like this. In her bed. She wanted kisses that never stopped. Wanted his hands on her body.

Urgency deepening the kiss and blurring her thoughts, she ground against him, pushing her fingers through that unruly hair. Gasped as his hands ran down her side, under her T-shirt.

Aching for him to touch her breasts, she arched her back.

Then the shrill buzz of her phone cut through the soft moans and kisses and her senses returned.

Lachie.

They were supposed to be at the nursery, not making out like teenagers in an empty clinic.

Lachie.

He was waiting for them. They should be there playing families.

She pulled away. Jumped off Finn's knee. 'Hot damn, Finn. What the hell are we doing?'

CHAPTER EIGHT

'ISN'T THAT OBVIOUS?' He was making a joke, but she was definitely right. They'd got carried away. She wasn't listening as she snapped up the phone from her bag.

Meanwhile, he was barely capable of movement at all. Arousal had shot through him the minute she'd covered his hand and hadn't abated; in fact it still continued to flare inside his gut, his groin, his head. He wanted to take her there on the floor. Wanted to feel the soft weight of her against him. Pressure against his heart. In his heart. Wanted to be inside her.

Dumb idea. But the best one he'd had in a long time.

Now, here they were with the best kiss of his life wedged between them, feeding her anger at him and herself. And he still wanted to do it again. And again.

'Yes. Hi. Sorry, got caught up in things at

work. We'll be there in five minutes. As quickly as we can.' She threw her phone into her bag, dived behind the back of the reception desk for a carrier bag filled with plastic boxes and started towards the door, straightening her skirt and smoothing down her hair with a palm. Pity. She suited being ruffled. And he had barely started to ruffle her. She shook her head as if reading his thoughts. 'Come on. Come on. We're late. Not a good impression at all.'

Well, at least she wasn't overcompensating for his leg. She seemed to have forgotten all about it. *Good.*

Which was not how he was feeling right now.

He caught up with her and stepped outside the front door. 'Sophie, just calm down a minute.'

As she locked the door and activated the alarm he saw the shake in her hands. He'd felt that when he'd held her before. She was anxious, turned-on, maybe a little scared. Not of him, but of the idea of *them.*

God knew, she had good reason to be. Things hadn't exactly worked out well before. She was right; they needed to take a step back and re-group. But it didn't have to be quite so knee-jerk.

She was tapping her foot as he retrieved the bottle of white wine from the car. 'Are you ready now?'

'Sure. It might not be cold enough, though.'

'I don't care. We're very late, Finn. This is not how I operate.'

'We could tell them we were developing cordial relations between mother and father. Surely they couldn't complain about that?'

'This is not funny.' She stormed down the path and onto the pavement, took a sharp right turn and headed off ahead of him.

'It's the truth.' Although things had spiralled a long way from cordial, judging by her reaction. 'So we're running there, is that it?'

'I'm in a hurry. I don't know about you.' She pulled up short and glared at him. Her cheeks were still pink, her lips bruised and swollen from the kiss. Her hair was awry, despite her efforts. He didn't think he'd ever seen her looking more beautiful. 'We can't do this, Finn. Okay?'

'What? Go to the nursery?' He didn't understand. Things hadn't suddenly become so bad she suddenly wanted him completely gone. Had they?

'No. Us. The kissing. Flirting. Any of it. Because if it doesn't work out between us two, what would that mean for Lachie? He needs stable parenting. God knows, I never had it. How would he feel to be in the middle of a sour relationship? It's not fair on him.'

'We'd never do that. Whatever happened, we'd always be civil and never put Lachie in shooting range.' He started to walk. He had no idea where they were going but it felt better to be moving.

She fell into step with him. Although hers was a whole lot smoother than his limping gait. 'Trust me, people say that all the time and then do the opposite. I know. I see it a lot.' She turned her head to catch his eye, he presumed to make sure her point was hitting home. 'I also see separated people who co-parent well. People who put their children first and their own needs second.'

'Is that what you want us to do?'

She pursed her lips. 'It keeps everything simple. No mess. No fallout. Don't you think it'd be for the best?'

'I think kissing you all over again would be pretty damned good, to be honest.'

'Finn! Would you stop joking for a moment?'

'It's not a joke. It was a good kiss. Okay, okay,

sometimes I say things to make you laugh. Sometimes I just say things to make me laugh. God knows, life can be very tough otherwise.' But she was right and they needed to work together to make this acceptable and pleasurable for Lachie. He didn't need to be brought up in a battleground, he needed a family. Family wasn't something Finn had ever planned on, especially after the accident. Family meant people relied on you day after day, they invested. He didn't want her investing in him. 'But okay. We stepped over the line. Got a little too carried away.'

'So we're good?'

He sighed. 'Sophie, we're very good. That's the problem.'

'I bet you say that to every woman you sleep with.' She shook her head.

'There hasn't been anyone since you.'

'Oh.' Her head whipped back round to look at him. 'You expect me to believe that?'

'Up to you. But it's the truth.' He hadn't had the strength of character to bare himself to another woman and risk seeing the disappointment in her eyes as she looked at his leg. Hadn't the confidence in himself to find someone and

then be unable to give her what she needed—
his focus and attention and time. But, also, he
hadn't been attracted enough to anyone to try,
until now.

They'd reached the nursery, a detached white
bungalow a little back from the street. *Little
Acorns* was emblazoned across the gate in bold,
bright primary-coloured letters, across the front
of the house, across the windows and on a huge
banner outside the front door. Finn narrowed
his eyes. 'Great-looking place, didn't catch the
name?'

She nudged him and seriousness leached from
her. 'Behave.'

'I am doing.'

'Finn's in the zero to two room. Squirrels. Be
warned…it's loud.'

She pushed open a door and he was hit by
a wall of noise. Babies crying, adults talking,
glasses chinking, a soundtrack of high-pitched
kiddie music. He strained for a glimpse of his
boy. 'Where is he?'

Sophie grinned and he could see pride glow-
ing from her. 'His favourite place to hang out is
the sandpit. He likes the diggers and trucks they

have to play with in there. He's got a couple of friends he plays alongside with.'

'Alongside with? Does that mean he's not great at sharing or something?'

'Finn, he's one and a half. He's not at the mixing and mingling stage yet. At this age they just all play on their own, together. If that makes sense. Look, there he is.' He watched as she spotted Lachie, knee-deep in sand in the far corner of the room, and waved. Everything about her changed in an instant. It was as if someone had indeed waved a wand and she'd transformed. Smiling, vibrant. Bright. 'Hey there, wee man.'

Lachie dropped a blue truck and held out his hands to his mother with a grin, identical to the one he'd seen a lot of recently on Cal's face, that lit his features.

She picked him up and covered his face in kisses and whispered something to him. Lachie grinned more and nodded.

She pointed to Finn as he wandered over to meet them at the sandpit. 'Look, Lachie. Here's Finn. He wants to say hi. Can you say hi?'

Lachie turned his head towards Sophie's armpit and rubbed his forehead against her chest.

'He can be shy sometimes.'

Finn dug deep and waited. *Please say hi.* No matter how much he told himself it didn't matter if Lachie didn't take to him straight away, it did matter. A lot. Silly to set so much store on the little guy. But he couldn't help it. Didn't every dad want his kid to like him?

Sophie repeated, 'Say hi to Finn, Lachie. Look, he's saying hi to you.'

'He did it so well at the clinic when I gave him the stickers. He can do it again now.' That was the thing; the boy had seemed blissfully unimpressed or bothered when Finn had met him the first time. But now, did he somehow sense this was a big deal? A father and son moment that he didn't want?

Sophie looked over and nodded, eyes silently saying something he didn't quite understand. But Finn gently tickled the boy's ribs with one finger and said, 'Give me a high five, Lachie? Like last time?'

He stopped short of bribing him with more stickers just to get an acknowledgement. But slowly Lachie turned to face him and raised his little fist.

He did it.

'Yo. High-five, dude.' Finn fist-pumped the boy very gently, showing him what to do.

Geez. First thing to teach him: how to be gangsta. He'd never live it down.

'Hi, Sophie. You made it.'

Finn swivelled to see an older woman in a very prim jacket and tweed skirt peering over.

Sophie smiled. 'Hi, Elaine. Yes, we had a bit of drama at work. Sorry to be so late to the party.'

'Not a problem. As you can see, we're nowhere near finished. Your boy's pleased to see you. He's had a good day today. Ate all his lunch and tea and played very well.' Elaine laughed at Finn, who was still stuck on high five variations. Making Lachie laugh too. He was making his boy giggle and chuckle and ask for more! *More!* Finn felt the woman's eyes on him a little longer and then she asked, 'And this is…?'

Sophie caught Finn's eyes as he stopped playing. What would she say? She opened her mouth, cheeks burning. She surely must have thought this through? He stuck out a hand and said, 'Finn. I'm Finn. Nice to meet you.'

'Hello, Finn.' Her handshake was exactly as he expected. Firm.

Sophie explained, 'You'll be seeing Finn around a bit from now on. I'll make sure he fills out all the correct forms in case I need him to pick Lachie up or do drop-off or...'

'I see.' Elaine looked over to Finn again and he wondered if he measured up to her standards. 'If you come through to my office some time before the end of this evening we can go through it all then. Just routine.'

And with that she turned on her low heels and went to talk to some other poor bloke. 'Is she the headmistress? Because she's a bit Professor McGonagall.'

'Oh, yes. She keeps the parents on their toes.' Sophie grimaced. 'I'm sorry. I didn't know how to introduce you. Lachie's starting to repeat things he hears. He probably wouldn't understand the words but...'

But I'm his father.

'You don't want him to say Dad and get used to the idea until I prove I'm going to stick around.'

'Two outings isn't a lifetime commitment, Finn.'

'I'm trying here. I can't suddenly fit every-thing into ten days. Tell me what more I can do.'

She looked up at him and her gaze softened. He could see the struggle in her eyes. The mem-ory of the kiss. The wanting. The knowing it was stupid to go there, but wanting to do it again anyway. He understood that she was torn in so many directions and that, for her, the hardest choice was to start to trust him.

She'd be wise not to.

He wasn't that reliable guy who would be there when needed. He had form, history of choosing himself over others.

'I know this is out of left field for you, Finn. You got up last Monday morning with no idea your life was going to change so much.' She put her free hand on his arm and leaned a lit-tle closer to speak, her scent bombarding him, stirring the desire again. He wished they were alone. Wished they didn't have this barrier be-tween them. He wanted to start again with the kissing. And this time to not stop. Her breath feathered across his throat. His concentration was shot whenever she was around; he couldn't focus on the important things. Well, other than kissing her—that was very important. 'I know you're trying hard, Finn. I can see that. And you're handling it well.'

He'd handle it a lot better if he didn't like her, didn't want her. 'I'll go fill out those forms. I know there'll be sections about my relationship to the child. You need to know I won't lie.'

'I don't want you to. But I'll ask them to keep the knowledge low-key until Lachie understands. Okay?' She nodded. Decision made. Everyone at the nursery would know he was Lachie's dad even if Lachie didn't. It felt like fireworks were going off in his chest. 'We'll be waiting here for you. Oh—do you think you'll need my help with any of the information?'

He patted his jacket pocket where he had the picture Lachie had drawn for him back when he was just the nice guy at the clinic. Finn's gut tightened that he needed a piece of paper to know the intimate details of his son's life. Details he should know by heart, have lived through. 'I'll be fine.'

'Yes. You'll probably just need to fill the bottom section of my form.'

'And you'll probably need to sign to say I'm legit or something.'

'Okay, do what you need to do and I'll get this boy settled in the reading corner. Which is…' she pointed to an area with low white bookcases and beanbags '…over there.'

When he returned from Elaine's scrutiny he found them curled up on a huge green beanbag, holding a book between them. Lachie was turning the pages and Sophie was saying the words in a sing-song voice.

His chest expanded and filled with light.

Soft idiot. This scenario had never been on his radar. Not once in his life had he wanted this. Rugby, mud, glory, beer, messy uncomplicated sex: that had been his life for so long. Then the hard route of recovery and wondering if his life was over.

This. *Wow.* This was altogether new. He hadn't realised what he'd been missing. But, hell, he'd missed the best part of living.

She turned and smiled. 'Hey. You found us. We're reading a story. How did it go?'

'Elaine's just waiting for your signature to say I'm trustworthy.'

'Did you get the headteacher beady eye?'

'She's a tough nut to crack, but when I said I was Lachie's dad she actually smiled. She didn't ask me much though.'

'She wouldn't. She's the height of good manners.' Sophie wriggled off the beanbag and said to Lachie, 'Mummy's going to talk to Elaine but guess what? Exciting! Finn's going to read you a story. You can choose which one.' She winked at Finn as Lachie stayed exactly where he was and didn't cry out for his Mama. 'Winning, see? If you slide your hand the other side of the beanbag you'll find I've poured two glasses of wine. Lifesavers when he wants you to read the book for the tenth time and you're bored out of your skull. Just a life hack from someone who knows.'

He watched her walk away, watched the swish of her curls, the sway of her backside and wanted to run after her and drag her into the store cupboard and kiss her senseless. *Stop it, man. Close yer mouth.* It wasn't right to think such things with a bairn close by. Was it? 'Right then, Mr Superhero. Which book do you want to read?'

Lachie pointed to the one Sophie had left on the beanbag so Finn picked it up.

But Lachie kept his distance, watching Finn holding the book. *Geez*, if he thought he'd had a breakthrough with the high five game he was certainly wrong.

'Come here, Lachie. We can read it together.' Finn held his breath as the boy shook his head and dropped his gaze to his shoe. He hit the trainer and it flashed. He looked back at Finn. Waiting. For?

Finn caught up. 'Ah. Your trainers. You remember I like them?'

The boy still didn't say anything. But he hit his shoes again and they flashed red. He looked up at Finn.

Finn's heart nearly exploded. His kid didn't know what to do or how to act either, but he wanted to make this man smile. 'Yep. Superhero trainers. I remember.' He had an idea. Stupid, maybe. But it was worth a try. At some point he was going to have to breach this issue; it might as well be done now as part of play.

Glancing round to make sure no one was looking, he rolled up his trouser leg and exposed part of the carbon fibre pylon attached to his prosthetic foot. 'Look at this. Half man, half robot.'

He tapped the pylon and gestured to Lachie to do the same. The boy frowned and wiggled his fingers over Finn's shoe and slowly tiptoed them to touch—so carefully—Finn's artificial leg.

'Tickles!' Finn drew his leg away. Feeling nothing, but feeling everything just to see his son interested and giggling. Lachie reached out and touched it again.

'Gentle. I'm very ticklish.'

Lachie snatched his hand back, eyes huge. Then gingerly reached out and patted Finn's leg again. This time Finn let him explore a little more.

It took a few minutes but Lachie's interest gradually waned and he seemed keen to read the book. So Finn encouraged him to come sit next to him and they opened the book together.

One step nearer. And yet Finn felt as if they'd conquered Everest. Lachie had taken it all in his stride and had even been so unimpressed he'd got bored. If only adults could treat his amputation the same way instead of making it a big deal.

This was the big deal: his son in the crook of his arm, the sweet baby boy scent, the cute curls, the profile of the little nose and long, long eyelashes. The concentration as he followed the words and nodded at the cadence. The next generation of Bairds. His son. Real live flesh and blood and, as far as he could see so far, brave and empathetic too. Sophie had done a great job, but now it was time for him to step up too.

This was real.

The lump in his throat almost cut his words off. But he forced them through. He was reading a story to his son, who seemed entirely happy to be here. All he needed now was Sophie on his other side, wrapped against him, and things would be perfect.

And now he was really in Dreamland. Because not only was it the furthest thing from her mind, it was also the most ridiculous thought he'd had. One kiss did not make a family; one kiss had, in fact, put a wedge between them.

Pity, because given another chance he'd do it all over again.

CHAPTER NINE

SOPHIE WATCHED AS Lachie tapped Finn's artificial foot then work his way up the carbon fibre pole and chuckle. It looked like something from a sci-fi movie, all black and silver and shiny with a skin-coloured foot encased by a shoe. Any adults seeing it would've been hard-pressed not to stare but Lachie seemed to be taking it all in his stride. But kids were like that; they accepted differences, barely even noticed them. Her heart stalled. This was the breakthrough Finn had been hoping for.

She craned her neck to have a better view of his prosthetic, then thought better of it. It wasn't her business. Instead, she watched them settle down together and then Finn turn the pages and say the words. The way he looked at his son almost broke her heart in two. He was invested and trying hard. That was something. A beginning.

The kiss had pushed everything from her memory back into reality. The past and the present were getting dangerously blurred. He'd tasted exactly as she'd remembered. And even though she'd only spent one night with him she remembered the way he kissed too. Remembered the way he'd made her feel.

Even though she was enjoying his company, she couldn't help feeling panicked that this was all happening too quickly, that they needed to slow things down.

He seemed to be aware she was watching, turned and waved, which made Lachie look up and come running over and the book reading was abruptly over. 'Sorry, I didn't mean to disturb you.'

'He likes me.' Finn looked as if he'd been given the best Christmas present ever. 'I think.'

'Of course he does.' How could he not? 'I told you it was just a matter of time. But don't be put off if he starts to gravitate to me again. He's tired and likely to get clingy.'

'And kids always want the familiar when they're tired, right?' But she'd broken the spell for them and now Lachie was stretching his arms out to be picked up by her.

Finn twisted to get himself out of the bean-bag; for most people it would have been an easy manoeuvre, but for him it looked difficult. She should have thought about that and chosen a more comfortable chair. But then he'd have hated that she was thinking of concessions for him. She turned away so as not to be seen watching.

Once he was upright he laughed. 'Everything is so much easier with two legs. If only I'd known before. Can I walk home with you guys?'

She tried to crush the uplift in her heart. It wouldn't do to get too involved. But she seemed unable to stop it. 'Sure. But your car's still over at the clinic.'

'It's not far; I'll walk over later and get it.'

'You can do the boots and bars tonight then.' She added an evil-sounding laugh. 'My first night off. Ever.'

'I'd love to. Anything to help.' Again with the Christmas present smile. Which did nothing to calm down the hitch in her heart and the desire to be with him, to spend time with him, no matter how much she knew it was a very bad idea.

She grinned, knowing the hullabaloo waiting for him with the boots and bars. 'You won't be thanking me later, trust me.'

They were home in no time and it felt surreal and yet somehow right to be showing Finn how to bathe and get his son ready for bed. How easy it would be to allow herself to fall into a kind of dream here. The perfect family.

Until he changed his mind.

Finn was laughing as he poured water over Lachie's head and rinsed away the bubbles. 'What a waterbaby. You just love it, don't you?'

Sophie took a step back and, with mixed feelings, watched the bond between them tug tighter and tighter as he lifted Lachie out of the bath, all dripping wet and covered in soap bubbles, and wrap him up in a warm towel. 'Right then. What's next?'

'Boots and bars, then bottle and then bed. It's a regular routine, same thing every night, then he knows it's time to sleep. No messing.' She handed him the warmed sipper cup of milk and as their fingers touched their gazes met over Lachie's head.

'Thanks, Sophie.' Finn smiled softly. 'I mean it. Thanks for this chance.'

'Don't thank me yet. You haven't done the boots and bars.'

His fingers curled into hers and longing wove through her, deep inside, making her lean towards him. Wanting him. Feeling too many things: a chance to find bone-deep happiness in his kisses, however fleeting, a threat to the status quo she'd worked so hard to achieve as the only parent to her adorable son. She didn't know the answers—if there even were any—but she'd bet that mooning over Finn wasn't part of the equation. She breathed out, let go of his hand and went through to Lachie's room and waited for them to follow. 'We usually sit on the floor for the boots and bars; it's easier.'

'Cool room.' He glanced round, eyes wide. 'Did you do all this?'

She felt a stab of pride as he noticed the pale grey and light blue paint on the walls and ceiling, the jungle-themed mural with a lion and giraffe keeping watch over Lachie's white wooden cot, the dip of branches from a tree heavy with grinning monkeys. 'Yes, it was great fun doing it. I knew I was having a boy so my friend Hannah and I decorated it before he was born.'

'It's exactly what I would have chosen. Although I don't have an artistic bone in my body.' He clambered down to the floor, left leg sticking out rigid as he leaned onto his hands, then twisted his body down. Everything he did required extra effort and forethought. That had knocked out the immaturity in him, for sure. But it hadn't diminished him in any way.

She tried not to look at the strength in his arms and upper body, tried not to imagine those hands on her face, on her skin. Or that smiling mouth on parts of her that hadn't been kissed by anyone but him for years. She picked up the boots and bars and handed them over. 'Right then, do your best.'

'Dickers.' Lachie tugged at his mum's arm and pointed to the drawer she kept them in.

'If you're a good boy and sit nicely, you'll get stickers.'

'Me?' Finn pointed to himself. 'Excellent. I love stickers. I can sit very nicely and I can be a very good boy...'

She knew he could. And a deliciously bad one too. 'Finn Baird, I swear—'

'Dickers. Mine.' Lachie's bottom lip began to tremble.

'Oh, dear. This may turn ugly. He's a bit fractious. It's quite a bit past his bedtime.' She grabbed the stickers and held them out to Finn, pushing back the memory of the teasing in his eyes. Trying not to recall the way he tasted. 'Right, boots and bars on then you can choose a sticker.'

Lachie shook his head.

'Lachie, mate. Boots and bars first, then stickers. I won't have any, they're all for you if you're a good boy.' Finn held out the boot for Lachie to slip his foot into. At least she didn't have to go through the motions of showing him how they worked.

'No.'

Sophie made a face. 'This is what it's like. One day he's great with them, one day he isn't.'

'That's toddlers for you.' Finn shrugged. 'Go pour the wine; I'll stay until he does it.'

'Are you sure?'

'Rough and crunchy or smooth and silk, it's all part of it. I'll sit here and wait all night if I have to. Go. Go put your feet up.'

'Really? Wow.' And boy, that was the last time she had to be asked. This was a glimpse of how different things could have been; a shared load, shared life. But she'd decided she wasn't going to dwell on that any more. She was just going to take advantage while she could. 'Okay. I'm out of here. Don't take any cheek and don't give in. The Chardonnay will be ready when you are.'

As it was she'd only polished off one glass of wine before Finn appeared in the lounge. 'I'd give anything for him not to have to wear those boots.'

'I know. Broke my heart at first too. You want them not to have to struggle. The endless plaster casts were a challenge too.' She tapped the sofa for him to sit and then handed him a glass of wine, which he took with a smile. It felt altogether strange, good and weird, that they were doing this. 'Only a few more years and he'll be fine.'

Finn's eyes blazed. 'He *is* fine.'

'You know what I mean. You want them to be...' She didn't want to say the word because it didn't describe what she really meant, but he guessed anyway.

'Perfect? No one's perfect, Sophie. I mean, not even me…damned close but…no dice. Or, rather, no left leg.' He used his humour as a shield, she could see that now. Always making fun of himself, to put others at ease. Getting the words in before anyone else had the chance to.

'I didn't mean perfect. I meant…it's hard for me to watch the other kids running around with no issues when we have this rigmarole every night.'

He shrugged. 'He probably won't even remember when he's older. He's hitting milestones, you say? He'll just be one of the boys. He'll rise above it all and achieve great things.'

'Is that how you feel about what happened to you? That you've risen above it? Got over it?'

Finn shook his head. 'I'm not one of those who thinks it's a good thing in the end that I lost my leg and that I see life differently now, that I appreciate things more. Like those people who say, *My life is better because of it. I really grasp every second now.* I was always grasping at everything, Sophie. I did grasping like a pro. I took everything for granted, the fact I could run and jump and grasp and grasp again at success, at life. Now I just have to grasp further and hold on tighter.'

'I can see you doing that. You're different to when we first met. More intense somehow. Same...same but different.'

He shuddered. 'Ugh. Sounds depressing.'

'No, actually. I think you're remarkable.' *God*, she sounded like she was his number one fan. She realised things were going down a mutual appreciation route she didn't want to take so she quickly changed the subject. 'Where do you live now? I don't remember you being from Edinburgh; weren't you just visiting? From near a loch somewhere?'

'I was born in a tiny village called Duncraggen at the tip of Loch Lomond, did most of my physiotherapy degree in Glasgow and then completed the rest by distance learning when I moved to Aberdeen to play for the Swans. The day we met I'd travelled here with the team for a game.'

'And you found me to keep you company while they went on to a club.' And they were both struggling with the consequences. 'So where do you live now?'

'Heriot Row. Ground floor apartment.'

One of the better places in the city. 'Very nice.'

'Not affordable on a physiotherapist's salary, but I did earn decent money playing rugby before the accident. I'm not rich, but I have more than enough.' He became a little more animated. 'I want to talk to you about that. We need to talk about financial support for you and Lachie.'

She didn't want to know where this was going. 'I don't need anything. I haven't got the authorities chasing you up for maintenance payments or anything.'

'I want to help out. I have money. I want to give you some. For Lachie. For you.'

'We don't need anything. We're fine.'

'You said you wanted a holiday. To travel. I could pay for that.' He was really excited by this.

It would make things easier, but she didn't want to be beholden to him. 'We're fine.'

His voice deepened and he frowned. 'You may be *fine* but everyone wants something. The only thing I want right now is to provide for my child.'

'I don't want your money. I didn't tell you about him because I wanted your cash. I told you because it was your right to know him.'

'He's my child. I want to support him. How

do you think I'd feel if you won't let me get involved at all? It's what people do.' Not letting him contribute was a challenge to his manhood, to his male pride, she could see.

'It's what *couples* do, Finn. People who've had a relationship breakdown. We didn't even have that. It was one night.'

'Whoa.' He jerked back in the seat as if she'd slapped him. Things were deteriorating. Fast. But instead of snapping back at her he took a couple of beats to compose himself. 'Yes, and that was because of my oversight. I need to make amends here. I can't make up for the last two years but I can make the next ones easier.'

'You have to stop trying to overcompensate for what happened. I haven't even thought… it's all so complicated. Jumping ahead. Too far ahead.'

'I'm not going to let you fob me off on this one, Sophie. I'll set up an account in his name and put something in every week and I'll set one up for you too and put money in there and you can use it for whatever you want. Holidays—that's what you want, right? He needs to have sun and sandcastles and buckets and spades. Ice cream

for afternoon tea and fish and chips out of paper.'
She could see the longing in his eyes as he said
those words. He wanted to do that too. Because
his father hadn't been around to do that with
him and his brother. He wanted to do all those
things his father hadn't done, to give Lachie everything he hadn't had.

He was shaping himself to Lachie's life, to his
heart and to his love, and she was suddenly ter-
rified and awed at the same time.

Would he be the one taking Finn away? From
her?

Would she be left behind? She had never con-
sidered being apart from her son, had never
missed one night of his life. She couldn't bear
the thought that she might miss him doing something fabulous, or something just mundane or
silly or…being left on her own. Or being beholden to someone financially, having to take
them into account with her decision-making.
She was losing control. Losing a little of her relationship with her boy possibly too.

Tears sprang to her eyes and she fisted them
away.

But Finn caught her in the act. 'What's wrong?'

'Nothing. I'm just tired.' And overwhelmed. She couldn't say any more. It wasn't her place to deny her son a fun time—to deny him the things she couldn't give him—but it didn't mean it hurt any less.

They sat for a moment in silence and she wondered how they could navigate through this and make things better. Time, probably. Maybe a contract would be a good idea. Her brain was muddled, mainly by the intensity of her attraction to him. By her desire to do right by all of them, and also by the threat to the independence she'd forged that meant she could call the shots about what happened to her and her son. 'I just want him to be happy.'

'Me too. We'll work it out.' Finn turned to face her on the sofa and took both her hands in his. 'I can see you love him so much. I just want to do the same.'

'Lucky boy.'

'You don't want to share him?'

He could see right through her. 'I'm scared what that means. For me.'

'He can love us both without one diminishing the other. Sophie, I know you didn't have the best time growing up without your parents, but we don't have to be like them, or like my own useless father. We can make this work. I'm not out to hurt you. Far from it.'

'I know.' He didn't want to hurt her but someone would be hurt.

'Let me show you.' He tipped her chin up and pressed a soft kiss on her mouth. And instead of pushing him away she wrapped her arms around his neck and pulled him closer. Seeking comfort from his heat. And that was the thing; she could be frustrated and angry at him and yet also deeply connected to him.

It was as if they'd been set on a predestined trajectory that nothing and no one could stop. He tugged her close and she could feel the heat of him. It didn't seem to matter that they'd agreed they couldn't do this. Neither of them could stop. She wanted to be here with him. She wanted to fit into his arms, to mould herself to the shape of him, and into his heart. Just for long enough.

However long that would be.

As long as Lachie didn't get hurt. She would never let that happen.

At the thought of her beautiful son sleeping

upstairs she pulled away. If she wasn't strong enough to stop this for herself, she could be strong enough to stop it for Lachie. 'This is too complicated, Finn. We agreed. I can't see anything clearly at all. Nothing. I want you in ways I didn't imagine, but I'm too scared to go there. I want you in Lachie's life, but not at a cost to me. Or to him.'

'I want all those things too. I also want to kiss you again. For a long time. I want you, Sophie. So badly it's like an ache that won't go away.'

This was too much for her to deal with. Bad enough she wanted him, worse that he wanted her too. But lust was like a shiny new present, easily dulled over time by overuse and familiarity. True unconditional love took time to grow and came from mutual trust. 'We agreed we shouldn't.'

'We can un-agree it too. We make the rules.'

'Don't make this harder than it already is, Finn.' She shook her hands free and went into the kitchen, switched the kettle on, kept busy. Because not being busy with Finn around was far too much temptation. 'I think we have to be firm with ourselves. If we keep giving in to this then one of us is going to get hurt. Or all of us. Because, be honest with me…do you see a long-term future thing here? Or has your head not worked through all that yet? Because it's all very new right now, but trust me, getting up in the middle of the night to a sick child, not being able to go out when you want, having to pre-think about every potential eventuality is damned hard.'

'You don't think I have to think about every eventuality? You think I can just jump up and dash out the door without planning ahead?' He shook his head. 'You don't know me at all, Sophie. You still think I'm the immature guy who's going to run, don't you? You don't think I can do this long-term. That I have some fantasy idea about being a father? That I can't do it.'

'No. I just—'

'You just don't trust me. Right?'

She didn't know how to respond to that. Because she wasn't there yet, but she was learning to let go, learning she had to. 'I want to trust you.'

Hurt was written in the lines around his eyes, in the way he took a deep breath and shuddered out the exhale. In the swift turn of his body away from her. In the grip on the table top to steady himself. In his voice and his words. 'Glad that's clear then. I'll be in touch about access to my son.'

CHAPTER TEN

TRUTH WAS, FINN didn't trust himself either. So, in many ways, she was right; they needed to keep this all above board with rules and guidelines so they both knew where they stood. Something to bind them all together, which was what he was doing now at the end of a busy shift. A week since Finn had left her house and he hadn't contacted Sophie, apart from a daily text asking about Lachie. Nothing else. No flirting. Nothing.

It was killing him. But it was the right thing to do.

'Bad day?' Ross stood in the doorway of Finn's office as he did every evening, assessing, checking in.

'Just getting a few things sorted out.' He still hadn't mentioned his relationship to Sophie and Lachie to his boss; better to keep things quiet until they'd nutted out the details. He sent the email and closed his laptop, girding himself for the reaction he'd get. But it was what she'd been hinting at. It was a start, anyway, to making things crystal-clear between them. Maybe then they could start working on the trust thing.

Ross coughed. 'I said...pub?'

'Yes, actually. I do need a pint.' Having talked to clients all day, what he really craved was some alone time, but he knew it wasn't what he should do right now. Being alone wasn't good for him. Cal would be proud he had such personal insight.

Ross grinned. 'Well, what are we waiting for? My round, and perhaps this time you'll actually turn up?'

'Try stopping me.' But as they walked down the hospital ramp and into the damp Edinburgh evening he couldn't help looking over his shoulder for a woman with caramel eyes and a heart of endless depths.

She wasn't there.

Two pints later he shoved the key into the lock of his house and dashed in out of the now lashing rain. His phone was buzzing with Cal's ringtone but he ignored it. What could he tell him? Things weren't working so well between him and the mother of his child. They'd muddied everything with a kiss. Two kisses. His self-control had let him down again.

He slumped onto the sofa, dragged off his prosthetic and liner and rubbed the pain away. Tried to.

The doorbell rang.

Damn. He'd expected a reaction, but not so soon. Maybe by return email. A grumpy text. Definitely not in person. He reached for the liner and fumbled to pull it on. Failed. Threw it back on the sofa.

'Finn! Open the door. I know you're there.'

The lights flickered and thunder crackled overhead. It felt like the thud of his heart. It felt like the end of the world, the beginning of hell. But they needed to go through this so they could come out better.

'Finn! I'm getting soaked out here. Open the door.'

He didn't have time to mess about with his leg. She'd have to take him as he was. He had no secrets. It wasn't as if she was going to see the scarring anyway; his trouser slipped down and over the stump.

Grabbing his crutches, he made it to the door

by the time she pressed the bell a third time. 'Sophie.'

'Finally.' The caramel eyes were a dark fire of molten gold. Water dripped from her hair; she had no raincoat, no umbrella, just a sweatshirt that was soaked through and jeans that stuck to her like plastic wrap. Shivering, she dug deep into her voluminous handbag and pulled out printed documents and waved them at him. The rain beat down now, thick and fast, and the paper started to wilt in her fist. 'What the hell is this?'

He moved aside and let her into the hallway, skin prickling just at seeing her, heart beating triple time, and it wasn't because he was worried about her reaction. He was worried about his own. How could he find an angry woman such a turn-on? He tried to focus on more important things. 'Where's Lachie?'

She glared at him. 'In bed. At home with Hannah. What the hell is this, Finn?'

He needed to stay calm. 'The start of negotiations. I just got a lawyer friend to mock something up so we could start setting out what we expect from each other.'

She shook her head. 'I can't afford to pay someone to do this. I thought we could talk about it one-to-one. An informal agreement. Why did you have to do this?'

'Because if it's written down then maybe you'll believe I have Lachie's long-term welfare at heart.'

She pointed to a paragraph she'd highlighted in orange and held it towards his face. 'You want him to stay over at your house? Here?'

'Yes. When he's ready. When I'm ready. Only on occasion. I'm not asking for joint custody or anything extreme, Sophie. I just want to see him.'

Her nostrils flared, her eyes blazed. Her mouth screwed up. 'I'm so damned angry with you.'

'I can see that.' *God*, she was magnificent. Heat prickled through him, made him hard. He wanted to absorb all that energy of hers in a kiss, in passionate lovemaking. He wanted her more now than he'd wanted anything in his whole sorry life. 'This is what you wanted, Sophie. This way you can hold me to my word.'

I've missed you.

He felt it resonate through him.

He'd missed her and he wanted so badly to hold

her, kiss her. To give in to the need that misted everything when she was near. Even when she wasn't. He wanted to let that need overtake them both, give in to it and stop fighting.

'No, Finn. Oh—' Only then did she seem to realise he was standing with a crutch shoved under his armpit. She looked at his trouser leg and shook her head quickly. 'This isn't what I want.'

So that was it. The heat seeped out of him. She was angry. She was scared. She was repulsed. The trifecta of doomed relationships.

Leaning on his crutch, he stumbled through to the lounge, expecting her to follow. It wasn't a pretty way to move, but he had to get her out of the cold hall and into the warm open-plan lounge-diner. They needed space. Walking over to the dining table, he flicked the top of a whisky bottle and poured out two fingers for each of them. Handed her a glass and leaned against the heavy wooden table. Steady. Belying his raging heartbeat. 'What do you want, Sophie?'

Her gaze caught onto his as she took a sip of the honey-coloured liquid and put the glass back on the table. 'I want to scream at you so damned loudly, Finn, for doing this.'

'Go on then. Scream.' He probably deserved it.

'No.' Eerily quiet, she crumpled the paper into a ball and threw it to the floor. He caught her arm, tugged her to face him. Her breathing was ragged. Despite the cold, heat radiated off her. This wasn't about the contract he'd sent her. Not at all. This wasn't about his leg. It was about the need between them.

'What do you want?'

'You've turned my world upside down. My head's all muddled. I thought it could be straight-forward. I want it to be.'

'Which is why I've found someone to help us clarify everything. I don't want emotions getting involved in our decision-making, not where our son is involved.'

'Everything I do for that boy is chock-full of emotions. I can't see clearly where he's concerned. He's been my first and last thought and almost every thought in between every single day for over two years. He's part of me, Finn. He's my everything. But you're…well, this is the bit I struggle with. I was angry with you for so long and I didn't expect you to be like this. I didn't expect to feel the way I do.' She put her hand to Finn's chest. 'So I don't know what I want. I don't want to be confused and angry, that's for sure. I don't want us to communicate through lawyers. I want us to talk. I want—' Her fingers curled into the fabric of his shirt. 'I want—'

'I want you.' She'd described exactly how he felt—even after such a short time of knowing he was a father—confused, muddled and too attracted to Sophie that it made his head hurt and his heart ache. The emotion in her voice was thick and raw and it seemed to reach deep inside him. It took all the strength he had to ignore it. 'But that's not good for either of us.'

Her fingers relaxed against his heart. 'I know you'd make me feel good, Finn.'

'I can't give you what you need, Sophie. I can't make a whole load of promises for ever and ever. I'm not that man. You almost said it yourself. You can't trust I'll be there for you. Hell, *I* can't trust I'll be there for you. Not long-term. Not happily ever after.' If anything showed up his weakness and lack of self-control it was her. This need. Now.

'Maybe this is the way forward. Maybe it isn't. But I don't think we can do anything but go with it. Tonight. Now.' Her mouth was inches away from his. Her eyes sparked a dare and a promise. Her tongue ran along her bottom lip and that almost undid him. 'Now, Finn.'

I want you.

Unable to resist any longer, he tugged her close, slid his hands around her waist. For one short moment he gave her time to pull away, saw the hesitation in her eyes, then the hunger. Saw the moment she stopped fighting. Then he pressed his mouth to hers, branding her as his.

She tasted elemental, of tears and rain. Of something new and fresh and yet so familiar it felt as if she were part of him. The kiss was soft at first, exploring, relearning. Then, as need unravelled inside him like ribbons of silk, they kissed harder. Deeper. Her fingers gripped his hair as her tongue danced with his in a messy open-mouthed kiss. Finding each other again. Searching new places. Feeding an insatiable

hunger. He didn't know how long they stood
entwined together but he didn't want it to end.

'God, Finn. Yes, I want you. I don't want to.
But I do.' Her breath came quick and fast as she
fitted her body against his. He felt the damp
press of her breasts and his hands found their
way there. Over her sweatshirt, then under. Slid-
ing his fingers under the straps, he unclipped her
bra, palmed a nipple and groaned at the pebbling
under his fingertips.

She shivered under his touch. He shifted
against the table so she could step in between
his thighs. Moaning, she rubbed her core against
his hardness but then she suddenly stopped kissing him and pulled away. 'Are you okay here?'

With the lack of leg? The subtext was glaring.

He closed his eyes against the rage of shame
firing through him. No one had ever asked him
if his body could handle this before. No one had
asked if he could manage the act, or even make
out. He fought back the strangling irritation in
himself. He looked over at the sofa and the cast
away pylon, the liner, and felt inadequate. Why
the hell had he taken them off? She wouldn't
have seen him as anything less if he was stand-

ing on two legs, even if one was false. He tried to keep the tension out of his voice, but knew it was still there. 'I'm fine.'

She looked up at him and smiled. 'You're making me very hot, Finn Baird, but I'm soaked through and starting to shiver. Can we…can I…? Where's your bedroom? I need to get out of these wet things quickly and under covers before I catch pneumonia.'

Touchy bloody fool. 'I thought…never mind.'

'Finn.' She followed the track his eyes had made and she sighed. 'You think I won't find you attractive?'

'You don't want me to screw up your life, Sophie. I can't give you what you need.' Therapy had taught him that his missing leg was an external metaphor for the missing internal part of him. The part of him that had made him choose his friends over his mother, made him fight his brother just to prove he was right. *That* was unattractive.

But she palmed his erection and all logical thought was lost. 'I want you, Finn. You. Not select parts of you. I want all of you.'

He needed her to be sure. 'When we first met

I was in peak condition, Sophie. Plus, I had two legs.'

'Pretty good condition, as far as I can see. Besides, I have stretch marks now; I've changed a lot too. People do, over time. You said no one's perfect, Finn. You hold that standard up for just you? Because from where I'm looking you're the closest to perfect I've ever seen.' She ran her free hand over his pecs. 'Will it hurt you in any way?'

Hurt? This was paradise. Her hand was still rubbing his erection and he was so hard he couldn't string two thoughts together. 'I don't know. No. I can't see how.'

She pinged the button on his trousers, slowly tugged down the zip. The anticipation of her fingers on him made lights flash behind his eyes. Then reality hit and the firmness of her hand around his naked flesh had him muttering soft curse words. It had been so long and he was too damned hard—it'd be over before it began. He moved her hand away. 'Give a guy a chance. Sophie, please. I want to kiss you everywhere first.'

He bent and gently caught her bottom lip be-

tween his teeth, then slid his mouth over hers
again. Somehow he managed to strip the sweatshirt from her damp skin. Threw the bra to the
floor as she peeled his shirt from his back.

'Just look at you.' She dragged her mouth from
his and kissed his collarbone, his pecs, sucked
in a nipple and made him shudder with white-
hot lust. 'Bedroom?'

'Too far.' Grabbing his crutch again, he walked
to the sofa and with one motion of his forearm
swept everything to the floor. From the arm of
the chair he grabbed a thick tartan blanket and
wrapped her in it and laid her on the cushions.
Perching his bad leg on the sofa and taking all
his weight on his good one, he wriggled the wet
jeans from her legs, leaving her naked except
for her panties. Goosebumps dimpled her flesh.
But, God, she was beautiful. 'I'll kiss you warm
again, Sophie Harding.'

'Do it. Do it now.' She threw the blanket over
him too and giggled, wrapping them close and
hot.

He didn't need two legs to give her pleasure.
Pressing her back against the cushions, he kissed
a trail down her throat as she arched against him.

As he reached her breasts she moaned soft and low and he nuzzled there until she was pulsing against his leg. Pleasure sparked deep inside him, spurring him on, making him drunk on lust, on the taste and the feel and the smell of her, melding her indelibly in his brain and in his heart as the connection tugged tighter into a desperate, ragged insatiable need.

His trail went lower until he reached her hip bones, kissing across the delicious dips and curve of her pubis. With one flick of his hand the panties were discarded and his fingers probed into the soft, wet depth of her core. He ran small strokes with his thumb over the tight hard nub and felt her contract around his fingers.

'Finn.' Her upper body lifted from the cushions as she thrust her fingers into his hair. 'Finn. I can't… Don't stop.'

'I'm not going to.'

'Oh. Oh… I need you inside me…' He felt her fingers grow slack, her head fall back and her core clamp tight as she moaned loud against the pillow. She enslaved his thoughts—his body was hers—and he knew that whatever she commanded he'd do it, willingly.

* * *

She'd never felt so desperate, so turned-on. A couple of moments, three, she was sitting up and tugging his face towards her for a greedy hot kiss. Then her hand travelled south again, slipping his trousers off, then his boxers. As his erection slipped free he groaned into her mouth. He was so hot. So hard. And she couldn't wait another second for him to be filling her. 'Condom?'

'Wallet.' He reached backwards and grabbed his wallet from his trouser pocket. From this vantage point she could see the side of his left leg. The missing space.

When he turned round he caught her looking. He shook his head and twisted so she couldn't get a direct line of sight to it. 'Don't. Just don't, okay?'

'You're beautiful, Finn. Magnificent.'

'Don't look at it.' He tugged her face so she would make eye contact with him. 'I want you, Sophie, so damned much. And I want you to want me. Don't spoil the moment.'

'Finn, your body turns me on. *You* make me feel so much. Too much that I'm scared. The way you survived your accident and what you've achieved since makes you more of a man, not less. Let me in.'

She clamped her eyes shut and fought the way he'd sneaked under her skin, through her bones and into her heart and wondered whether he'd ever feel the same about her. Whether she was making another mistake by being here with him. But she couldn't do a damned thing about it; she was in so deep. She couldn't help but be honest; this wasn't a time for holding back so she kissed him, opening her eyes and looking only at him, at the bright shimmering blue of his eyes, at the face that had melted her resolve that first night and still did so today. At the man who was the father of her son, a part of her life. A piece of her heart. And she told him through that kiss exactly how much he turned her on, what she felt.

By the time they drew breath he was hotter and harder and his breaths came in gasps. 'Are you sure?'

'Hell, yes.' She pulsed against him, trying to assuage the need between her legs, the sexual frustration rumbling through her body as it ached for his touch. Then he was sheathed and above her and his eyes were burning and yet misted and she could see the same out of control desire she felt mirrored there.

She shifted her hips and felt the hard length of him fill her, whip her breath away and fill her with heat and light. She clenched around him and he gasped again, pulling out almost…almost… then thrusting into her again. She matched his rhythm, hooking her legs around his thighs and pressing her body full against his so she could feel the solid fast beat of his heart and inhale the masculine scent of him.

He groaned into her mouth and she felt him shift sideways and the pressure lessened. Another stroke and the pressure mounted again— he was playing her like a musical instrument, building to a crescendo she didn't want to wait for.

'Can I…? Can we…?' She wriggled out from beneath him and sat up, then straddled his thighs, positioning herself over him.

The mist in his eyes cleared and for a moment she thought he was going to stop.

But she found his mouth, caught his gaze then slid over him, rejoicing in the way he filled her like no man ever had. 'Don't you remember? Last time?'

'How could I forget?' His smile was all sex as he tugged her legs around his waist until she was sitting on his thighs, her face touching his face, her breasts touching his chest. Skin against skin. Mouth against mouth, until she didn't know where he finished and she began. He rocked into her. Harder and faster. She could barely form words, definitely not thoughts, as pleasure tightened deep within her, threatening to burst her heart wide open. 'Oh my God, I can't…this is… perfect.'

'Yes. You are.' He held her face as he crashed into her over and over. He held her gaze as his eyes widened and he groaned loud and strong, her name over and over. Sophie felt wave after wave of light thrumming through her as they reached the peak together. And she knew that whatever happened next, however their lives unfolded after this, she would never be the same.

CHAPTER ELEVEN

FINN LAY BACK on the couch with Sophie wrapped over him and tried to catch his breath. Tried to make sense of the swirling emotions in his chest.

So much for him having changed, having wrestled his self-control into submission and being the big guy who thought of others first. No matter how mind-blowingly brilliant making love with Sophie had been, this had no doubt thrown them into more confusion. But, even so, he wouldn't change a thing; this time with her was a gift.

She pressed kisses along his collarbone and up his throat and sighed against him. 'Well, that wasn't what I came here for. But I'm very glad I did.'

'Me too.' He kissed the top of her head and squeezed her closer. 'I need to get you angry more often.'

'No, thanks. I prefer to keep my blood pressure within normal limits.'

'Mine's sky-high right now. The things you do to me.' He kissed her again, then latticed his fingers with hers as she rolled off him and settled against his side. He was drawn in by the golden hues in her eyes as she smiled at him. Satiated. Breathless. Beautiful.

Lachie had his eyes. Her smile. The best parts of them both. They'd created something so perfect and now this…her. Reaching heights he'd never thought he'd go to again. A solid heat settled under his ribcage and his mind cleared. For the first time in a long time he felt complete. As if, in this very moment, he had everything he needed.

How long would it take for him to blow it? 'So, why did you choose Lachlan out of all the names in the world? Is it your dad's name?'

She shuddered at the thought. 'No way. I wouldn't name him for his grandfather. Lachlan means from the land of the Lochs. Warrior. It was used to describe the Vikings when they invaded. I thought Lachie may need to be a warrior one day; having a strong Scottish name would be handy. I also—' she stopped '—nothing.'

Finn was more than intrigued. 'What? What were you going to say?'

'Nothing.' She kissed him again and he wondered how it was she knew exactly how to turn him on. How to fill the need and stoke the fire at the same time. It was as if she had a direct line to his very core.

'Don't think you can fob me off with mind-melding magic kisses.' He stroked her hair, unable to remember a time when he'd chosen to lie with a woman and just talk…except the last time with Sophie. 'Tell me what you were going to say.'

She smiled. 'Okay… I remembered you said you were brought up near a loch. It seemed fitting.'

Fireworks lit up his solar plexus. 'You named him for me?'

'In a roundabout way, I guess. Loch boy.'

Even though she'd been angry and confused and hurt, she'd clearly been determined not to pit her son against his father. She hooked her leg round his good one and the rub of bare skin made him prickle all over with heat. One look, one touch had him burning with desire. He was destined to want this woman for ever.

'And Spencer? What's that about?'

'Don't laugh, but my grandma had a cat called Spencer when I first moved here. I loved him the minute I met him. He let me do those horrible things kids do to their pets, like dress them up, or carry them like babies. He was very tolerant and very calm and I hoped Lachie could be a little like that too. Calm, but wise. A warrior when necessary, but also quiet when needed.' She laughed. 'He's got a fair bit to go yet. One day, maybe.'

'He's named after a cat?' Okay, so now she was a little crazy, but he loved it.

'It's his middle name, but yes. Why not? A lovely cat with an awesome temperament and he was brilliant at catching leaves.'

Yes. Crazy. 'Good call, then.'

'You wouldn't have called your son after a cat?'

'Hey, I had a cat back in Duncraggen called Fidget, not really the name for a boy.'

'Actually, the perfect name, but I think he

might get ribbed at school for it.' Her stomach growled and she rubbed it, laughing. 'Oops. Sorry.'

'Hungry?'

'Ravenous. I missed dinner somewhere between getting your email and waiting for Hannah to arrive to babysit. I was too angry to think about eating.'

'Like I said. I should get you angry more often.' He slid out from underneath her. 'Stay right there.'

'Yes, boss.' She gave him a salute and collapsed back into the cushions.

The goosebumps were back on her arms, her hair still damp and forming little curls that framed her face and made her seem younger somehow. He tugged the blanket around her. 'I'll put your clothes in the tumble drier. Should be dry by the time we finish eating.'

She sat up again, the blanket wrapped around her breasts. Still modest after everything they'd done. 'But I can do it—'

'Sophie—' he cut her off '—it's just food and washing. Simple. How do you think I manage day to day?'

Turning away from her, he reached out and picked up his liner and prosthetic and dragged them on, hoping she couldn't see what he was doing. Then he pulled on his trousers, bundled up her wet clothes and got the hell out of the room. It wasn't that he was being helpful so much as it was a good excuse for some headspace.

She'd called their son after him, even though she'd been angry and hurt and confused. They'd kissed each other naked, shared the most intimate of lovemaking. But even now he needed to take his time before showing her his leg and she felt embarrassed with him seeing her naked.

All the desire and need in the world couldn't make up for the depth of intimacy time brought with it. They'd taken steps into the unknown here tonight, but they were still new to each other in so many ways.

His head was whirling as much as his chest. Too much too soon? Unspoken promises he didn't know if he could keep?

Once he'd finished piling things onto a tray he steadied himself and balanced it in one hand while he used the crutch for his other.

She was still sitting up when he came into the room, still wearing the blanket as she eyed the food greedily. 'Finn Baird, you're a domestic goddess.'

'I try my best.' He set the tray down, then went back to the kitchen for a bottle of wine and two glasses. The half-full whisky glasses twinkled in the light, catching his eye as he walked past the table. Had that only been an hour before? So much had happened between them since she'd stormed in all wet and fierce and he'd thought he might lose her altogether.

He poured the wine and slid onto the couch, the tray between them as they tucked in to olives and French bread and cheese.

'This is exactly what I needed.' She wiped her mouth on a napkin and sighed. 'How long will it take for my clothes to dry? I should really think about going soon.'

His gut tightened. He wasn't ready to say goodbye yet. 'I wish you could stay longer. You wouldn't stay the whole night last time either.'

'Finn Baird, you know the rules. You never sleep over the first time.'

'And you wouldn't let me take you home.'

She shrugged a shoulder and tore off a piece of bread. 'Taxis are always easier. Trust me, I didn't want to leave. I just thought I should.'

He should have made her stay and spent the next day with her too. Things would have been so different. 'I remember feeling two distinct ways as you left—empty and lost that you'd gone. And so excited that I had your number and would see you again. You made me happy for the first time in months. I just wanted more of you. Of what we'd shared.'

She put down the bread and nodded for him to continue talking. 'So walk me through that next day. What happened?'

It had been an idle reminisce; he hadn't meant to turn the conversation down this route. 'It's ancient history. Boring.'

She shook her head. 'It's filling in the gaps for me, Finn. I often wondered why you didn't call. You stood me up. You pissed me off. My whole life changed. So tell me…so I can fit the pieces of the puzzle together properly.'

She had a point. He owed her an explanation. 'I think I told you a bit about my mum when we were in the bar. That she'd had a stroke and died a few months before you and I met?'

'Yes. You were really cut up about it when we started to share our sob stories over too many shots of tequila.'

He laughed. 'A sob story. That's one way to describe it.'

Sophie's eyes softened and she covered his hand with hers. 'You really loved her.'

'I did. But not enough. In the end.'

'That's not who you are. Why would you ever think that?' She had a way of asking that seemed to promise she wouldn't judge. He wanted to tell her. Tell someone. Sometimes he felt as if he was carrying a huge weight in his gut and maybe talking to Sophie could help with that.

'When I first started to play for the Swans I was the golden boy. Everything I did worked. On and off the pitch. Everyone loved me. The team, the boss. Women.'

She flicked her free hand at his. 'I do not need to know that.' She pigged her eyes. 'Was I a groupie, Finn? That's what you thought?'

He laughed. 'You can't be a groupie if you

don't even know who the guy is, Sophie. That's not how it works.'

'Oh. Okay.' She shrugged again. 'That's a shame. So tell me about being a golden boy; maybe then I can be a real groupie.'

'Oh, I think you could be now.' She was trying to make this easy on him, but he didn't deserve that. His gut clenched tight as he talked, guilt infiltrated his bones. 'I played well, scored a lot of tries, did everything right and loved the praise. I'm ashamed to say, I got a little cocky and narcissistic.' *A little?* 'One night I was playing close to my old home so I told Mum I'd be round to see her. She was so excited. But I got distracted with my teammates. We'd won a game and I was all cock-a-hoop and we were celebrating hard. I kept looking at my watch and promising I'd leave in a minute. But I never did. We went to a nightclub and my phone kept buzzing and I just ignored it.'

He shook his head. How had he thought he'd feel better giving voice to this?

'Finn…you were just a kid caught up in yourself.'

'Not such a kid, really. It was less than three

years ago, Soph. Turns out she'd had a stroke in the kitchen. She'd made my dinner, set the table. Then she'd collapsed and wasn't found until the middle of the night when the neighbours saw the light on and the curtains open. If I'd been there I may have been able to help her so much more quickly. Worst case—she had the stroke because she was so upset I hadn't turned up.'

'You can't carry that on your shoulders, Finn.'

The weight in his gut travelled to his chest and pressed down. Hard. 'I can and I will. I was selfish and stupid and self-centred and should have kept my promises to her. Instead, I chose to get drunk with people who I couldn't rely on when I needed them. I lost my mum because I couldn't give her what she wanted, couldn't put her first.'

She lifted the tray and put it on the floor beside them then edged closer to him, stroking his back. 'You're different now.'

He wished he was, but he was so stuck in getting by, getting on, he still wasn't sure he had enough space for anyone else. 'How would you know? When have you had to rely on me? When have I had to give you anything? You refuse money. Time with Lachie is managed. And trust…?'

'I trust you can do things for him, Finn. For us. We need to get to know each other better. Like this.' Her voice was soothing and silk to his raw one. 'Tell me about that night.'

'I'd rather not. I'd rather talk about you. Or, even better, I'd rather…' He reached for her and pulled her onto his lap. 'I'm done talking for tonight, Soph.'

She put her hands on his shoulders and pressed him back against the arm of the couch. 'Finn Baird, you are strong and wonderful and funny, but there's a part of you that's still lost in the dark and needing light. I know there's a bruise on your heart and I want to rub it clear away. But the only way you can help is to let it go. I'm here, it's okay. Let it go.'

She wriggled closer and kissed him deeply. And again. Kissed him until he couldn't think straight. The only thing he knew for certain was that he wanted to be inside her all over again. And he knew she wanted him there too. He thumbed her bottom lip. 'I'd much rather do this.'

She shook her head. 'We're honest, you and I.

That's just one thing I like about us. Don't hide from me. Let me in.'

He kissed the tip of her nose and then tapped his heart. 'You are in.'

The smile she gave him at that admission had a direct line to his chest. 'So talk.'

'Not tonight.'

'Then I'll go. Are my clothes dry, d'you think?' She edged away.

'No. I doubt it.' He took a deep breath and blew it out slowly. She wasn't going to let him get away without offloading some of his story. If keeping her here meant talking, then he'd talk. 'Mum's death was just the start of things going wrong. I was grieving and angry and made some bad calls on the field. The harder I tried, the worse things seemed to get. I went from golden boy to water boy in a matter of weeks. And the guilt over my mum's death seemed to grow. I couldn't talk to Cal about it. I couldn't talk to the boss because it wasn't the kind of thing you did. So it started to eat me up from the inside. Then I met you. The one shimmeringly good thing about those few weeks.'

'You didn't tell me this at the time, though.

You just said you knew how I felt about my grandma dying.'

He smiled, remembering how much he'd wanted to impress her that night in the bar. 'Hardly the greatest chat-up line: *I think I killed my mum.* Besides, you actually seemed to like me. I didn't want to jeopardise all that. You were amazing. This shining golden star in the midst of a whole lot of crap.'

'But you kissed me goodbye, said you were going to be busy and you'd call me in a couple of days. You never did. I take it you saw Cal the next day and did the hike?'

'Yeah. We'd planned it a few weeks before. I think he wanted to check how I was. He's always kept watch on me, like a father figure. I guess, being the older brother, he felt it was his job. Still does. We both wanted to climb Ben Arthur again. So we set off. I was in a foul mood. And tired.'

She grimaced. 'My fault.'

'Not at all. Seriously. I think I was just completely wiped out by all the guilt and emotion. We trudged to the top pretty much in silence. I was going to tell him everything—I wanted to—and I'd just about got the courage up when it started to snow. It went from clear skies to a whiteout in a matter of minutes. We lost our bearings and started to argue. I lost it. He lost it. Two angry men filled with grief and testosterone and pride. Not what you want at the top of Ben Arthur in a storm. He wanted to go in one direction, I wanted to go the other. Both of us believed we were right.' Finn hauled in air. Two stupid pig-headed men.

'Not ideal.'

'He was shouting at me. I told him he didn't have to think he was always right. That if I wanted to do my own thing I could. So I started to trudge down one way in the snow. He came after me and told me to grow up and that we had to stick together. Things got bad. I told him he was jealous of my success. I said some stupid stuff that I'd been bottling up—all the anger poured out of me, towards him and towards myself.'

'You were hurting, Finn. Sometimes we lash out when that happens.'

'He said he would never be jealous of me. That I was an idiot and he'd had enough of looking out for me. Sibling stuff. Nothing important and yet...'

He drew in a deep breath. 'I see things differently now, but in the heat of the moment when I was hating myself I thought he hated me too. I thought everyone did. I thought I'd killed my mother, let the team down and in a blinding flash of clarity I thought things would be better for everyone if I didn't exist.'

'But you'd just spent the night with me. You knew I didn't hate you.'

'Logic says yes. I couldn't stop thinking about you on the drive out to the mountain. But by the time we were lost up there all the good vibes had gone and I was cold, hungry and angry with big brother. So, Cal's next to me, grabbing my arm, trying to pull me to go his route. I'm pushing him back and I can see the edge of the mountain looming up towards me. And beyond that it looked like there was nothing there. Just nothing. And for one minute that was what I craved. Nothing.'

She looked at him, open-mouthed. The pain he felt deep inside was written in her features. 'What are you saying?'

'That I still don't know whether I lost my footing or whether I stepped out into thin air on purpose.'

'Oh, darling.' She took his face in her hands and kissed him hard and it felt like some kind of forgiveness. Absolution. 'I can't imagine how that felt.'

'Trust me, you don't want to be there.' He couldn't even put it into words. 'I woke up on that ledge, dazed and confused and shivering and in so much pain. Everywhere. And my brother talking non-stop to keep me alive. I knew then it was what I wanted more than anything too. I've been fighting my way back ever since.'

'Thank God you survived. Look at you. You're magnificent. You can do anything.' She paused and thought for a moment. 'But when I found out I was pregnant I searched for you everywhere. I looked online and I never saw anything about you and the accident…'

'I insisted it was kept low-key, out of the news as much as I could. No names.' He looked at what was left of his leg. 'You think I wanted this broadcast to everyone?'

She ran her hand down his thigh and to his

knee. Then over his knee to where it stopped. 'Does it still hurt? Phantom pain, that kind of thing?'

He took her hand away from his knee. 'I get it occasionally. I still forget I don't have the damned thing from time to time too.'

'Can I see it?'

He closed his eyes. Exposed both inside and out. And some of that old exhaustion bit him again. 'Why?'

'Because it's part of you. Because I want to prove to you that I think you're amazing, what-ever your leg looks like. That I know you can do amazing things.'

'Another time, eh?'

'Finn. It's me. We've just shared something… I can't even describe it. My heart feels so full.'

'I know.' He cupped her face and kissed her. But he wasn't ready to open himself up to such scrutiny yet. 'Not today, Soph. I can't.'

She shivered and dropped her gaze to her hands. 'Okay. That's okay.'

But he knew he'd disappointed her. 'Another time. I promise.'

'It's okay. Honestly.' The invisible lines tugging them closer were starting to fray and if showing her was the only way to mend that, he'd do it. He began rolling the trouser leg up but she stopped him. 'No. You're right. I'm pushing you too much. It's all happening too fast.'

'It's okay. Look. Let's just get it over with.' He bent towards the trouser leg again.

But this time she shook her head and pulled his hand away. 'Stop it, Finn. I don't want you to do it like this. I'm sorry.'

He didn't know what to say or do as the warm bubble around them popped, covering them in a confetti of awkward silence. 'So. You want more wine? More food?'

Her phone buzzed and relief flickered across her eyes. 'That's probably Hannah thinking I've got lost or something. You know what? I really should go.'

'I'll drive you.'

'No. It's stopped raining. I need the fresh air and exercise.' She leaned in and kissed him. Squeezed his hand then slipped off the sofa, wrapping the blanket like a shield across her body. 'Don't get up. Text me later. We can arrange another time to get together. If you still want to?'

'Sophie, don't get the wrong impression; of course I do. I just don't want to do a show-and-tell right now, okay?'

Showing her meant opening himself up to his absolute most vulnerable. It wasn't about the way it looked. Okay, it was…but it was also about the way it made him feel. A symbol of all the stupid decisions he'd made. She was one of the better ones and he didn't want to risk what they were growing. Although he had a feeling it might be too late.

She came back into the room a few minutes later, dressed back in her jeans and sweatshirt. She waved as she left. No more kisses. And his heart began to stutter.

Truth was, it wasn't Sophie who had problems with trust. It was him.

CHAPTER TWELVE

SOPHIE WAS TRYING to concentrate. But everything seemed so muddled today. Ever since she'd left Finn's flat two days ago she'd been out of sorts. He'd bared his soul and she'd got all sniffy and tried to push things instead of letting him take his time.

Texts back and forth had been friendly enough but she knew she'd overstepped and it seemed as if the emotional reaction to having him in her life had become physical; she couldn't stop her heart from racing and her hands from shaking. Which was difficult when she was writing up the results of a hearing test on a toddler.

She looked over at Jackie Campbell and smiled reassuringly at the anxious-looking mother. 'The glue ear is all healed up and Billy Junior is doing just fine.'

Relief shone on the woman's face. 'So he's not deaf?'

'All the results today are within normal limits. He may get glue ear again, but we'll keep monitoring him. If it does come back and starts to affect his learning or speech, we'll have to think about inserting grommets. But that's down the track.' The shaking wasn't going away and now it was accompanied by a thumping headache and a raw throat. Not a physical reaction to Finn, after all. Still, she had enough of them to keep her body on alert. She tried to focus on Jackie. 'So, how are things at home?'

Jackie smiled, the most relaxed Sophie had ever seen her. 'Better now we've got a good routine sorted out and money to spend on food.'

Something going right for someone. Good. Jackie deserved some happiness. 'How's Billy? Have you heard from him?'

'He's doing okay. He's called a couple of times, when he's allowed to. It's hard for him, but he's committed. I've never heard him sound so determined.'

'That's good.'

'Can you thank that man again for me?' Jackie stood and beckoned to her boy to come over and take her hand. 'If he hadn't sorted out that place for Billy I don't know where we'd be.'

'Finn? Yes. I will.' And there she was, thinking about him all over again. Trouble was, she couldn't stop and it was getting in the way of everything. 'Have a nice evening, Jackie.'

'Thanks. You too. You look a bit pale. You okay?'

'Just tired, I think.' Sophie waited for her clients to leave, then pulled out her phone and did a quick check of her face in the camera app. Her eyes were glassy and her cheeks bright red. *Ugh.* Not a good sign.

A sharp rap on the door had her stuffing the phone back into her bag. 'Come in.'

'Sophie? Ready to go?' Finn stood in the doorway and her heart raced in a *pleased-to-see-you* tattoo.

'Hey there. Yes, I'm done.' And strangely, physically, she felt it too. Completely done in. 'Let's go get the boy.'

But he didn't move and there was a strange look on his face. One she couldn't read. Was he having second thoughts about what they'd done the other day? Was he feeling backed into a corner? That wasn't a conversation she wanted to have but they had to broach it.

He gave her a kind smile. 'Having another difficult day?'

'No, actually, it's been okay. Jackie said to say thanks for getting Billy a place at the Rose Clinic. He's doing well.' She ran a hand round the back of her neck, suddenly feeling hot and cold at the same time.

'Yes, I saw her on the way out. You okay? You look…how best to say this without you taking it the wrong way?' He came into the room and held his arms for her to step into. 'Very beautiful, but tired.'

'I'm fine.' *Beautiful.* She felt far from it. She felt befuddled and confused. She laid her head against his cool chest and wrapped her hands around his back. Nothing felt better than his arms around her, holding her…holding her *up* today. But she couldn't hide from reality for ever. 'Finn, we need to talk. About the other day.'

'Ah.' She sensed rather than saw tension capture his jaw. He shook his head. 'I was an idiot.'

'No, you weren't. I've been thinking—maybe we should slow things down a bit.' She unfolded herself from his arms, feeling the swift bite of space and cold away from his heat.

He took a step back, palms raised. 'You want to stop this…?'

'No.' Not with one cell in her body, but her brain had other ideas. 'But we can't fit the last two years into two weeks or even two months.'

'Okay. I can do slow. I like slow…slow kisses, slow dancing, slow sex…' Relief flickered across his eyes. His fingers played with the hem of her top and then tiptoed underneath and up towards her bra. She curled back into his touch. She didn't want to be apart from him, from this. 'I'm enjoying getting to know you.'

'The feeling is very mutual. But we need time. I shouldn't have pushed you.'

'Sophie, I was more than happy with everything we did. And, for the record, whenever you want a rerun just say the word.' He backed her against her office desk. 'In fact…are we the only ones here?'

'Yes.' She arched against him, pressing herself along his length as his hand covered her breast, wanting him inside her—her body hot for entirely different reasons now. It was so inappropriate to be doing this in her office, but she didn't care. And cared even less as his mouth found hers.

It was the kind of kiss that branded her as his. That wiped all sensible thought and made her legs woozy and her brain even dizzier. But she managed to drag her senses back when she clunked her elbow against her work computer and scattered papers across the floor. She pulled away, reluctantly. Hesitantly. 'We really need to stop doing this here.'

He straightened her top and smoothed down her hair. 'Yes. Lachie needs picking up; we don't want to be late again.'

The thought of her son had alarm bells ringing in her head. Or maybe that was the fog of headache that seemed to be getting worse, despite all the best kisses in the world. 'I think we shouldn't do this kind of thing when he's around. You know, the holding hands thing or kissing. Am I being presumptuous that you even want to do that?'

'Still protecting him?' Finn didn't answer her question, she noticed, as he gathered together all the scattered papers and piled them on her desk.

She should have filed them or something, but she didn't have the energy. She needed what little she had to get her point across to Finn and then whatever was left to walk round to pick up her son. 'I'll never stop protecting him. But I don't want him getting confused. Until we know where it's going.'

He tipped her chin up. 'Where do you want it to go, Sophie?'

To bed. For ever. To be in those arms, to kiss him and never stop. To feel the roughness of his jaw against her skin, to bask in the heat of those eyes. To soothe his grief. To share his worries. To raise him up. To share the wonders of their boy.

She wanted the works: everything he had to offer and more. But she knew what he had to offer might not be enough. That he was still healing. Knew, too, that fairy tales didn't happen, families didn't always end the way they started and that no amount of wishing could make dreams happen.

Mostly, she didn't want their son caught up in a war. 'I want Lachie to be happy and feel safe.'

So both of them could avoid the difficult questions. Another thing they had in common.

'So no holding hands or kissing in front of… anyone? That's what you want.' He ran his thumb across her cheek and anyone else would have thought he was on board with the idea but she could see he was stung by it.

'It is. Now we should go.' As she stepped forward the room blurred then eventually caught up, making her nauseated. 'Ugh.'

His arm slid round her waist. 'You okay?'

No. In so many ways.

Her head hurt and her heart didn't know how to act. 'Just a bit dizzy, you know. Nothing.'

'You're very pale.'

'A bug, I think. My throat's cracked and my head's pounding. I hope you don't get it too; I shouldn't have kissed you.'

'Oh, yes, you should have.' He fitted his hand into hers and walked slowly with her to the door. 'It's because you got wet the other day. I knew I should have undressed you sooner.'

'Yes, you were a bit slow on the uptake.' She couldn't help smiling at that. 'Really, I'm around littlies every day with their snotty noses and coughs. Lachie's at a nursery where every week there's a note about some bug or other going round—I think I've had just about everything in the book.'

'Maybe this is a new edition.'

'It's probably a twenty-four-hour thing. I just need painkillers and an early night.' She grabbed hold of the wall as the room swam in front of her eyes again. 'Whoa. Dizzy. Hang on.'

'I'm driving you home right now and you're not getting out of bed until I say so.'

'But Lachie needs collecting from Nursery.'

His eyebrows rose. 'Well, here's my first chance at being the pick-up dad. Do I look like I'd pass Elaine's inspection?'

'Yes.' He looked pretty damned eatable. Very determined. And a little out of focus. 'But I can—'

'I'm not taking no for an answer. You stay in the car while I nip in and collect him, then I'll do the bedtime routine. Okay?'

She'd miss reading her boy a story. Miss the cuddles. Miss the endless scuffle over the boots and bars.

Was this the beginning of the changes she was so afraid of?

Finn winked. 'Don't look so worried. I'll manage.'

'If you need me, you'll ask, okay?'

'We won't need you; we'll be fine.'

That was what she was afraid of. She bent and got into the car, let him pull the seat belt across her and closed her eyes to stop the world tumbling around her. He was being thoughtful and kind and exactly what she needed.

But not necessarily what she wanted. Oh, she wanted him with a force she didn't understand. But she didn't want a Finn-sized complication in her life. He was going to take over. He was going to be the last person her son saw tonight. He was going to reinvent the sweet routine she'd worked hard at creating. He was going to be with her boy and she wasn't, and she didn't have the energy to disagree.

Bath. Bottle. Boots. Bed. That was what she'd said the last time he was here. Or something like it. She'd made it sound so easy, but how did you do the kitchen thing without bringing the kid downstairs with you and all the problems that entailed? Conversely, how did you leave him upstairs on his own?

Finn had put his hand up for this without thinking it through.

Story of his life. Plain and simple: he hadn't a clue what he was doing.

His brother's face appeared on the phone screen. 'Morning. Evening. Whatever it is where you are. Not like you to call me. What's up?'

Finn shook his head. Yeah, phoning his brother was a surprise to him too. 'How do you make up a baby's bottle?'

'It says on the side of the tin.' Cal scratched his head. He looked weary. Unshaven. 'Wait. Are the bottles sterilised?'

Finn looked around the kitchen and didn't see anything that looked like a steriliser. Or a tin of milk powder. 'He's one and a half…do they need to be sterilised? Does he even need a bottle? I think he had a cup the last time I was here.' He should have paid more attention instead of goofing at Sophie. Right now he'd give anything to be goofing at Sophie—goofing with her instead of trying to work out a puzzle of his own making. Every thought he had seemed to be directed at her. She'd shifted space in his chest and stepped right in, but now he was walking into thin air and falling. 'Actually, yes, a cup. It was…plastic…yes. How long in the microwave to heat milk?'

Cal shrugged. He was in his own kitchen, across the world, shaking cereal into a bowl and splashing milk over it. 'How do I know? Look it up on the Internet.'

'Right. Yes. Good.'

Cal's laugh rumbled round the kitchen. 'You're looking after Lachlan on your own? Have you been dumped? Or just dumped in the deep end?'

'Sophie's sick. She looks terrible.' He was surprised by how the raw instinct to look after her had sprung out of nowhere. How, even after the confusion of the last few weeks, he still wanted her with a ferocity that took his breath away. The microwave beeped and he swivelled round to switch it off so as not to wake her. Twisted his leg. Bit back a shout. He didn't have time to be precious about his stump right now. He had other things to focus on. 'I'm being Dad. And not a very good one.'

He wanted to be everything she wanted him to be. She couldn't say it in words, but he saw the wistful look in her eye. Knew enough about her past to guess she wanted the happy ever after thing.

More than anything he wanted to promise her that, to make her happy for ever. But he didn't know if he could do it. He was still working on happy right now.

Cal laughed again. Heartily. 'Finn, you'll be fine. Just go with your gut feel.'

'Which is to hide in a wardrobe right now, exactly where my son is, refusing to do his nightly treatment for his feet.'

'Crawl in with him then.'

He shook the milk, tasted a bit to test the temperature. Tried not to heave. Hot milk. *Ugh.* 'I've left him upstairs. There's a gate on the bedroom door so he can't get out. There's nothing there that can hurt him... I checked and triple-checked. But I need to go back and deal with him.'

'Bring me upstairs with you. I've got to see this. You with a bairn. Plus, I want to meet my nephew.'

The stairs in this house were lethal. Steep. Narrow. Finn edged up them as quickly as he comfortably could and found Lachie exactly where he'd left him: in the wardrobe playing with wooden trains. Finn put the cup down and crawled in with him, then showed him Cal's face on the phone screen. 'Say hi to Uncle Cal. Do a fist bump.'

'He's only one and a half, Finn.'

'So? He's very advanced for his age.' Pride bumped in his heart as his boy lifted his hand to the screen and touched his uncle's fingers. 'Good lad. Now show Uncle Cal your stickers. Lachie gets them when he's a good boy.'

'Like now? He's being a good boy now.' Cal's voice changed from gruff Scots to a gentle burr Finn didn't even know his brother had. 'Show me your boots and bars, clever wee man.' And just like that Lachie tore open the Velcro on his boots and he slipped them on.

No arguments. No curled lip. No tears. 'See? He's very advanced for his age.'

'Precocious. Like his father.' Cal's eyes danced as he watched father and son. 'Nah, he's a good kid, Finn.'

Finn crawled out and beckoned to Lachie to come with him. Together they hopped across the floor to the cot. Man and boy with dodgy legs and crooked smiles. A pair from the same mould. Something deep and feral surged in Finn's throat. 'I'm going to read him a story.' If he could get the words out. 'So we'll go now.'

'No! Don't hang up. I want to say goodnight.' So Cal stayed with them through the bedtime story and even sighed as Lachie slipped off to sleep. 'I never thought I'd see the day where you thought of someone other than yourself, Finn.'

Ouch. But he was right. For the first time in his life Finn's first thoughts weren't of himself or his day or his future, they were filled with pride and excitement at seeing Lachlan and his mum. With trying to work out ways of convincing her that somehow he could be in their lives all the time instead of having to wait until the designated rendezvous day. And, always on the tip of his tongue, convincing her that spending another few hours in bed with him would be a very good idea. 'I think I'm falling, Cal.'

'Fallen, mate. A goner, I'd say. Not surprising, he's very definitely a Baird.'

I mean Sophie.

'Not just Lachie, though.' He tried to find the right words, deliberated, and decided to just say what was worrying him. 'She wants to see my stump.'

'So? Show her.' His brother's eyebrows raised. Nonchalant. No big deal.

'Just like that?' He made it sound so easy.

'It's who you are.'

'That's the problem.' He had to say it before he imploded. 'She might not want me then.'

'Ach, one day you'll realise you are so much more than what you believe yourself to be.' Cal looked at him through the screen, those Baird eyes as intense as that night in the snow when his big brother had convinced Finn to stay alive. 'Just stop fighting everything. You seem to think the accident was a penance for being a bad lad or something, but it wasn't. It was just an accident. You need to put your energies into other things now. Your boy, your family. Let yourself fall for them, Finn. Enjoy the ride instead of analysing it.'

Family. Was that what they were? Was that

what he wanted? Just the thought of it made him hopeful and panicked at the same time.

'I can try. I want to. Thanks.' One day Finn would have the guts to tell his brother about the night their mother died too. One thing at a time. A pint together in the same city would be nice. A pat on the back, a shared joke. For once the distance between them seemed too big. The floorboards in the room next door creaked and Finn's attention was diverted. 'I can hear her moving around. Got to go.'

His brother grinned. 'Aye, okay. Love you, honeypie.'

'Back at you, ya bampot.' Finn laughed and rolled his eyes. Things were starting to even out between them. About time too.

One problem solved. Now he just had to work out what to do about Sophie.

There was something cool on her forehead. Someone sponging her neck. Then a lot of shivering. Blackness.

Someone climbing into bed and holding her close, stroking her back, pulling the covers over her when she was trembling with cold. Stripping them off when she was too hot.

Someone tugging off her damp T-shirt and helping her on with a fresh one. Giving her sips of water. Holding her steady as she fumbled her way to the bathroom.

Someone kissing her forehead and telling her to go back to sleep…not to worry.

A lot later she was aware of light filtering through the curtains, an empty space next to her in the bed. And an ache for those arms round her again. She sat up, her head less muzzy for the first time in what felt like weeks.

The door creaked open and Finn stood there, a tray in his hand and a smile on his face. 'Hello. You're looking a lot better.'

'My headache's not so bad now.' If ever there was a remedy to illness, just looking at him smiling at her was it. But there was a piece missing. *Oh, God.* What had she been doing, sleeping in bed when she should have been taking care of her son? 'Where's Lachie?'

'Having a nap. He's fine. He's missed you, but we've managed.' Finn settled the tray on her lap. Opened a napkin and pointed to a bowl of something hot and steaming that smelt divine. 'Some chicken soup for you.'

He was surprising, this man. At every turn. 'More domestic goddess goodness. You made me soup?'

'Let's not break the spell with the truth.' He perched next to her on the bed and handed her the spoon. 'Not made exactly; I heated it up.'

'Packet?' She looked at the pieces of chicken in the thick broth and didn't care where it had come from, only that he'd thought enough of her that he'd done this.

'Organic and homemade, it said. Nice?'

She tried some; it tasted of garlic and rosemary. Of comfort and home. 'Yes. Delicious. Just like my grandma used to make.'

'You mentioned her a couple of times while you were sick.' He picked up the photo she had on a dresser. 'Tell me about her.'

'I miss her.' She took the photograph and ran her finger down the black and white image of her grandma, taken in the back garden of this ancient house, dressed in an old jumper and thick woollen trousers, spade in hand and smiling warmly at the camera.

Sophie's heart lurched. Maybe it was because she was still sick, but she missed her more today, not less. She had a feeling her grandma would have known what to do about Finn. She'd have told her not to be scared and to have an open heart. That Lachie had a capacity to love both parents equally. That loving one didn't mean there wasn't enough left for the other. Her grandma had had that capacity too; having already brought up two daughters on her own, she'd made a home for her granddaughter and never once made Sophie feel she was a burden. But Sophie knew that love could stop short. That wanting someone to love you and knowing they didn't was the biggest heartbreak of all. 'She taught me about unconditional love.'

'I'm sorry your parents didn't, Sophie.' He stroked her hair. 'She must have been very special.'

'She was. She was wise and funny and strong. She tried to protect me from the damage my parents wreaked, but you can't protect kids from everything.'

'Though you want to try.' He meant it, she

could see. He was living it. 'Sounds like she was a good woman.'

'She never said a word against them, but she supported me, listened to me, made me believe what I was feeling was legitimate.'

'Sometimes that's all you can do.' He fitted his fingers into hers and held her hand gently, and that gave her encouragement to talk.

'The first time they arranged to see me I sat in the lounge and waited for them for five hours. They never came. I got up the next day and waited again. My grandma never said a word, just fed me and made sure I got to bed. But on the third day I bawled. *They weren't coming.* She said they must have got caught up with something important. *What about me?* I screamed. *Aren't I important?* I heard her talking to them on the phone, insisting they come. But they didn't. It happened time and again, and if they ever did manage to come they'd be in and out in a matter of hours. Like I wasn't enough to keep them there. And each time they left it broke me a little bit more. I went from being this super-confident kid to a...weak one.'

She shivered. It was the worst thing. That and believing that if you wished hard enough for someone to love you then they would, in the end.

He tipped up her chin so she could look into those blue-blue eyes. 'You, Sophie Harding, are far from weak. You are formidable and strong and God help anyone who gets in the way of you and your boy. You love fiercely and that's not a weakness. That's the greatest strength there is.'

There was something missing from his words. His expression told her he wanted to be that. To have that capacity to love someone else. But he didn't think he could do it, she understood that now.

He didn't think he could, but love was in his actions, in the way he looked at Lachie. He loved his son fiercely already; he was just scared to let himself relax into it all.

They were matched in that then. 'Lachie's the reason I get up in the morning. My life's shaped around him.'

'You give him everything you didn't get from your own mum and dad.'

'I try to.' But she was still struggling to work

through the ramifications of Finn being in their lives and how they could, or even if they should, shape things around him too.

'Now, eat.' He made sure she ate every drop of the soup. Gave her a glass of water and made her drink it all. Then he slid down next to her and tugged her to him, his breath whisper-soft on her cheek. 'You had me worried for a while there.'

'Sorry. I was completely wiped out.'

'We coped, me and the boy. It was touch and go with the bedtime routine, but we got through. Lucky I'm a fast learner.' His gaze wandered over her face, settling on her eyes. He smiled and every cell in her body hummed for his touch. He leaned closer and pressed a soft kiss on her mouth, sending shivers of desire through her. It was exactly what she wanted, but he pulled away too soon. 'I needed that. Right, close your eyes and get more rest.'

She wasn't going to argue. Her bones still hurt. She lay back against the pillows and wished he was in here with her. Had she dreamt he'd climbed in and stroked her back? Or had that been wishful thinking? 'Yes, boss. What about you?'

'I have chores to do.' He picked up the tray and her heart stuttered. 'A man doesn't get to be a domestic goddess by sitting around chatting.'

CHAPTER THIRTEEN

THE BEDROOM WAS in darkness the next time Sophie woke. And she was alone. The old house was making its usual little night-time creaks and groans and she should probably have stayed in bed, but energy rippled through her and she needed to stretch and move.

Slipping out of bed, she tiptoed to Lachie's room and found her boy fast asleep in his cot. She kissed the tips of her fingers and pressed them gently to his head, unerring endless love spreading through her as he cooed and turned over. Her boy was safe. He was well.

Thanks to Finn.

She needed to see him, to say thank you. And more.

The lounge was lit by the orange glow of a lamp on a side table in the corner of the room. Finn lay fast asleep on the sofa, wearing a T-shirt and dark cotton jersey shorts.

Had he been sleeping on her couch the whole time? Had she dreamt his hands on her back?

At some point he'd been back to his house and gathered some things together: a small overnight bag with neatly folded contents, his crutch propped against the sofa arm. His prosthesis lay discarded on the floor, his damaged leg exposed. Heart pulsing at her throat, she stepped closer, tiptoeing so as not to wake him. Wanting to look. Wanting to get over the hurdle he seemed to think was insurmountable.

It was a leg that stopped just below the knee. That was all. With fading stitches and a neat fold. It was what it was. A leg without a foot. Not pretty, not ugly. Just what it was. She looked deep within herself, measuring her reaction. There was nothing. No emotion, apart from a deep sense of sadness about what he'd endured and that he was still dealing with the fallout.

He shifted on the cushions and seemed to sense she was there, even in his sleep. He sat up; immediately his hand went to his leg. He dragged a throw over it. 'Sophie? What's wrong?'

'Nothing. Nothing at all.' Her son was safe and asleep. She was feeling better. Finn was here, in her house. Everything was almost perfect. The one thing that would make it wholly so was him sharing her bed.

Sharing her life?

She was scared as hell about that.

He relaxed. A little. 'So, you're awake and it's the middle of the night.'

She knelt next to him, not looking at his leg or the prosthesis, just looking at his face. And wondering how just looking at a man could give rise to so many emotions. 'Yes. I'm wide awake. I feel like I've been asleep for years.'

He nodded, hand still on his leg. 'Three days, actually. You missed the whole weekend and a day at work. But you were clearly very sick. I almost called the doctor out, but you settled. In the end.'

'Three whole days?' Time had been a blur. 'Were you here all that time?'

'Of course. I phoned in sick for you this morning. And my boss is very understanding, although he was a little shocked when I told him about Lachie being my son. I've taken carer's leave today.' He was wearing it like a badge of honour, his back straighter, pride etched through his features. 'Didn't even know there was such a thing. How do you feel now?'

'I feel better. Cooler.' Determined to face the one thing between them, she pushed the cover off his leg and laid her hand on his stump. 'See. Cool.'

He twisted, his hand hard over hers, his voice a warning. 'Sophie—'

'I've already seen it. And you know what?'

'What?' His whole body stiffened. Guarded. Defensive. And it damn near broke her heart. This was a man who deserved so much and yet flinched at anyone getting close. He just had to let go. Let her in.

Let me love you.

The thought thrummed through her, unbidden. Uninvited.

No.

Loving him was a step too far. Loving him was a sure-fire way to breaking her heart.

She blinked as tears gathered behind her eyes. He was generous and funny and smart and a domestic goddess. How could she not love him?

She didn't want to love him. *But she did.*

Oh, hell. When would she ever learn? She loved him and he didn't want her to.

He didn't want to share his fears, his scars. He didn't want to let her in. Sure, he wanted to be a father to Lachie. He wanted to be part of this, but he didn't trust himself enough to be able to take that leap wholeheartedly.

Her mind whirled, trying to make a plan and to reconcile her thoughts and her emotions. She had to show him he could do it.

'It's just an amputation, Finn. That's what it is. And you're magnificent with it.' She'd liked him with two legs; she loved him with one.

Although, she doubted he wanted to hear that. She didn't want to believe it herself.

She placed a palm on his chest, ran her fingers slowly down to the soft arrow of hair on his belly that she'd seen when they'd made love. She felt him harden at her touch. 'I've run a bath… You want to come and share it?'

Hunger flared in his eyes but he shook his head. 'No. I'm great here. You go.'

Her body ached through to her bones for him, like the sickness she'd just been through: systemic and utterly consequential. The only way of recovery was through his touch, his kisses. 'Come with me, Finn. Let me in.'

Let me love you.

Refusing to take no for an answer, she pulled his face to hers and kissed him. Hard. Felt him hesitate then give in to the rush of raw arousal that was spiralling between them. Hot and hungry.

Eventually he pulled back and captured her gaze in his and she felt naked and exposed and beautiful. His fingers cupped her face and his next kiss was sweet and sexy and languorous as heat and need flared inside her.

Let me love you.

The words were on her lips and she fed them to him in snatched breathlessness until she felt him relax.

Let me love you.

She pulled his shirt over his head and pressed against him, fitting herself to him. Body to body. Heart to heart.

He stripped off her T-shirt and her foggy memory reminded her of a blurry time during her illness where he did the same to the soundtrack of soothing words. She didn't want comfort now.

She burned for him. She wanted him on her, in her. Now and always.

His hand was on her breast, then his mouth sucked in a nipple, and the only sound she heard was his name on her lips. The only scent in the air was of them. Of us.

She writhed against him, impatient and desperate. 'I need you, Finn. Please. Please. Come with me.'

His assent was more growl than words, but it was enough.

This wasn't happening. At least, couldn't be. Shouldn't be.

Finn was too drunk on need to resist. She drove him wild, made him want to do things he'd be better off not doing. Like this—sitting on the edge of the bath with her straddling him. Her hot mouth on his. Her damp core writhing against his erection.

His leg in plain sight. In all its messed up glory.

One minor shift in position and he'd be inside her. It was the only thing he could focus on.

But she stepped off his thighs and climbed into the bath, then took his hand as he turned and slid into the warm water to face her. Her kisses slowed, her touch became less frenetic, more reverent as she scooped water into a cup and let it flow slowly over his head, like an anointment. The soft touch of her fingers in his hair as she massaged added a surreal sensation of relaxation and intense arousal. Only Sophie could do that to him. Only Sophie…

He tried to take the cup from her so he could wash her too, but she stopped his hand and rinsed the soap away. 'This is for you, Finn. Lie back.'

Leaning in to kiss him, she ran soaped hands down his chest, across his belly. Down his thighs. Then she kept her eyes on his face as she slowly massaged down both legs. Inching closer and closer to his scars.

His gut twisted in anticipation and fear.

Stop. He tried to move away from her touch, but she shook her head, taking his left leg in her hands and kissing from knee to stump. He couldn't move without the risk of slipping or drowning. Hell, he was already drowning in her eyes, in lust with her. She paused. 'Does it hurt?'

'A little.' It was reddened by lack of rest but he

didn't care. He'd done what he'd had to do and been father to his son, helper to Sophie. *Lover.*

It was all he wanted, he knew that now. But after she examined his leg…he didn't want to imagine the fallout. Cal said he should let go. But Cal didn't wear these scars inside and out every day.

But maybe his brother was right.

Holding his breath, Finn hardly dared watch her expression as she reached the scar site. Saw no revulsion as she ran her fingers so gently across the bumpy skin, no grimace, no pretence of affection. She wasn't turned off. She didn't turn away. She accepted him.

Accepted him.

Hell, at least one of them did.

In her eyes he saw only genuine compassion. And need. And something he was not going to give name to because it was too soon, too intense. Even though he felt the same emotion flare in his chest.

He wanted to run. He wanted to stay. He wanted her.

Sophie's pupils were flecked with a shimmering gold as she smiled at him.'I want to kiss the pain away.'

He wished it could be that easy. 'I think that would work a lot better further up, honey.'

She laughed. 'Incorrigible.'

'Just being honest.' He pigged his eyes at her and laughed with her. 'A man can try, right?'

'I know exactly what you need.' Lifting his leg from the water, she kissed from stump to knee. From knee to thigh, eyes greedy and dancing and laughing and teasing. Hot waves of lust fired through him as her lips closed in and she took him in her mouth.

'Sophie,' he groaned as his fingers curled into her hair. It was almost too much. 'Sophie.'

He should have told her to stop. But the words never made it from his throat.

She didn't stop. She sucked him in, and again, and he couldn't stop his back arching as white light flared deep inside, building and building.

He was on the edge. So close. Her mouth so hot on his skin. Warm water soothing and arousing. Her breasts against his thighs.

But then she stopped, reached across to a cabinet cupboard, hands back to frantic as she fumbled with a packet. 'I want you inside me.'

'Trust me, there is no place I'd rather be. Ever.' He sat forward and pulled her to him, face to face, body slick against body. And she slid over him, moaning as she did so, rocking on him hard and fast. Then crying out as she rose and rose, taking him with her.

He crushed her against him, held her tight and let himself fall with her. Fall deep and hard and completely. His broken body, his heart, his everything.

It was late when Finn woke, entangled in bed sheets and Sophie's languid limbs. She was fast asleep, curled into his arms. The fever had definitely gone now and her chest rose and fell slowly.

His heart stuttered just to look at her. On her breasts he could see faint stretch marks. Tiny silvery lines that told of a woman who'd carried his child. Who'd fed their baby.

Geez. He wished he'd been around to see that. Now he had to make up the time.

He glanced at the clock and smiled. They were

going to be late for work and he didn't care. He wanted to do this all day and all night.

Her eyes flickered open and she sleepily whispered, 'Look at that. We managed a night together.'

'Rule-breaker.'

'I never thought I'd be called that.' She wriggled close and kissed him. 'Did you ever think this would happen? You and me like this again?'

'Never in my wildest dreams.' That was what this felt like: a dream. Any time now he was going to wake up and be alone and filled with self-loathing for the person he was.

But dreams didn't come with sound and smell. Dreams didn't come with the benefit of touch. He ran his hands over her silk-soft skin, running circles over her thigh and higher as she snuggled against him, moaning against his shoulder. Her floral shampoo scent filled the room as she kissed him with a need that matched his and, just as things started to get very interesting, the silence was crashed by loud wails coming from the room next door.

'Uh-oh. No rest for the wicked.' Sophie shrugged and moved away. He could see she was torn between her own needs and her son's. But he knew damn well she would always put her son before anything else. As would he. Now and for ever. Her hand trailed along Finn's thigh and she flashed a smile full of promises. 'I like being wicked, just so you know.'

Then she shimmied out of bed and pulled on a dressing gown.

Finn sat up and swung his legs over the edge of the bed. Still not wanting her to see what he didn't have, but feeling as if something monumental had changed for him last night. Sure, he didn't want her to see him like this, but he knew he was the only one who cared. She'd made it very clear she liked all of him and not just the physical.

Besides, he didn't want a minute without seeing her or his boy and if that meant his scars were visible then so be it. He reached for his crutch at the side of the bed. 'I'll get him if you like—give me a minute?'

She stopped at the door and thought. 'Okay. We normally have cuddles in bed first thing in the morning, but this *Mum and Dad under the covers* scenario might be confusing for him.

Bring him downstairs? I'll get the milk ready. And bacon sandwiches. You've done enough waiting on me; I need to return the favour.'

'Excellent.' So this was what a family was. His heart bloomed as desire made room for excitement, rubbing along with a deep feeling of being…happy. She made him happy. Sophie made his life so much better. He blew her a kiss. 'Have I ever told you how much I—?' He clamped his mouth shut to stop the words pouring out of him. *How much I love you.*

Hot damn.

Did he love her?

He wanted to. More than anything.

But it was stupid to think he could love her so soon. That kind of thing didn't happen. Not to him. Not to Finn Baird, who didn't know how to love anyone but himself.

'How much you love…?' Her eyebrows rose and uncertainty flickered across her face as she gripped the bedroom door handle. Uncertainty and longing.

Which almost shattered his heart. He couldn't promise something he couldn't give. 'How much I totally love bacon.'

'Doesn't everyone?' She breathed out and her gaze slid away for a second then back to him. 'Oh, and Lachie likes to manage the stairs himself. You just need to stand in front of him and let him slide down on his bottom.'

'Yeah. We've been doing races.'

'Of course you have. Men!' She rolled her eyes. 'Thanks for watching him. I'll make a start on breakfast.'

'I'll make a domestic goddess out of you yet,' he called after her, laughing.

'Takes one to know one,' her voice floated back as she disappeared.

Love was such a small word for a big deal. A huge deal. These two people were a big deal. This family.

He didn't know if he loved them yet, but he wanted to. After the accident he'd believed he was unlovable and incapable of loving anyone else, but she'd made him rethink that. He'd done some stupid things, shown nothing but egotistical pride and selfishness, and he'd paid a hefty price. Even so, she accepted him as a father to Lachie and as a lover. And God knew, he'd do anything…anything…for them.

That was a huge deal. A lot like love.

Still smiling, he walked through to Lachie's bedroom and helped him out of his boots and bars, then, balancing half on his crutch and leaning heavily on the cot sides, Finn lifted him out of the cot. Lachlan smelt of sleep and was probably still half in Dreamland as he clutched little fists round Finn's neck and cuddled into his neck. They'd come so far in such a short space of time. They had so many good years ahead of them but he couldn't wait. He wanted it all now.

He held the boy against his chest and whispered, 'Hey, good morning kiddo. Time to get up.'

'Finn.' Lachie grinned and put his finger on Finn's chest. 'Finn.'

'That's me.'

Daddy. One day he'd hear the word, when the time was right. He was okay with that; he knew who he was to his son, so Finn would do for now.

Nappy changed and standing on the carpet, Lachie held his arms out to be picked up again, but Finn shook his head and walked him to the top of the stairs. 'Nah, wee man, get your slip-slide on down the stairs. Mum's cooking. Come on, I'm starving.'

But Lachie stamped his foot and stood on the top step with his arms outstretched. 'Finn.'

Oh. Trouble on the horizon. What kind of a dad should he be? Authoritative? Stoic? A push-over? A friend? Would he ever stop asking himself that? Did anyone? 'On your bottom, come on, Lachie.'

'No.' His little arms stretched further as he tiptoed up towards Finn. The bottom lip started to curl and big fat tears started to roll down his cheeks. 'No.'

'What's the deal here, eh? The last two mornings you've wanted to race. Why not today?'

As if a toddler had any rhyme or reason for being contradictory.

'Okay, mate. Calm down.' The boy was still half asleep, and maybe he was getting his mum's bug. Who knew? Finn couldn't do anything but give in to him. The pull to inhale his boy's sweet scent again was too much. He picked him up and shifted him onto his right hip. 'One cuddle, then we're going down on our bottoms. It's not safe any other way.' He nuzzled against Lachie's head and felt emotion clutch his heart. He was besotted. For sure. 'We're on our way, Mummy. Get the bacon ready,' he called down.

'Finn!' Lachie pressed his hands to Finn's face and laughed, tears just a memory.

Unbelievable. He was too cute, this kid, and he certainly knew how to play the heartstrings.

'Right, time to sit down.' But as Finn bent to put Lachie down, the boy wriggled in the opposite direction, clinging to Finn's neck and scrambling up over his shoulder.

'What are you do—?'

Spinning off balance, Finn twisted sideways and forwards. Tried to catch the top step with his foot.

His goddamned *not there* foot.

Missed.

Tried again.

No. Hold the boy. Save the boy. Hold him.

And once again he was falling into thin air.

CHAPTER FOURTEEN

A SICKENING CRUNCH had Sophie running towards the stairs. The pained groans had her heart racing. Too fast. 'Finn? Lachie? Lachie?'

No. She didn't want to look, to know. Air stalled in her lungs, she couldn't breathe.

'Lachie? Finn?' Relief made her limbs weak as she found her little boy sitting halfway down the stairs, eyes huge and glassy, lip trembling. But whole. Then panic again, seeing Finn face down across the stairs, head and shoulder at a funny angle.

No. Her heart hollowed out.

Who to comfort first?

Finn made the decision easy. His voice, though muffled, was determined. 'Get him. Quick. Is he okay?'

Lachie's eyes were big and scared but he wasn't crying. Yet. 'I think he's in shock, but he looks okay. What happened?'

Finn slid himself upright onto the floor at the bottom of the stairs. He groaned and rolled his shoulder back and forth. She could see he didn't want to admit what had happened. To say the words.

'Did you fall or something?'

'Is he okay?' He groaned again as he shuffled up the stairs to check on Lachie. His hands ran over the boy's body, head, face. Checking. Worrying. Assessing. 'Did he get hurt? Are you okay, mate? I'm so sorry.'

'He's fine.' Thank God. She shouldn't have left them alone. But they'd been okay while she was sick. What the hell happened? This time she infused assertion into her voice. 'What about you? Are you okay?'

'I'll live.' He shook his head.

She didn't want him to just live. She wanted him to be the happy-go-lucky man he'd been ten minutes ago. The one who'd kissed her to sleep. She wanted him not to hurt. 'You don't look okay.'

'I'm fine.'

'No, you're not. Just admit you're hurting and we can sort it out.'

He turned away and checked his stump. Closed down and froze her out. Just like that.

'Finn. Look at me. It was just an accident.'

He carried on checking his body, rolling his shoulder. No words. Nothing.

She put her hand on his shoulder. 'Finn. Talk to me.'

'It was my fault.' He finally looked at her with hollow eyes and the burden he was carrying was almost palpable. 'Take him and give him something to eat. He's hungry and he's going to start grizzling.'

'But—' She stopped herself from pushing him for more. He was angry and sore and no amount of mollifying words were going to help, she knew that about him now. She picked up Lachie and squeezed him close. Kissing his face. Then bent to Finn. 'If you won't let me help...' *Or let me in.* 'Then at least tell me what happened.'

He huffed out a long breath and shook his head. 'Just take him away. I'll be through soon.'

But he wasn't. In the end she gave up waiting and fed Lachie. Managed to force a couple of mouthfuls into herself. Got her son ready for

Nursery and gathered her things for work. On autopilot.

She was in the hallway clipping Lachie into the pushchair when the sound of a bag zip flared a warning deep in her gut. Finn was leaving.

Of course he was; he'd only moved in to help her. But she'd allowed herself to believe beyond that. Idly wished he might just move more things in.

Slowly, she walked through to the lounge and found him sitting on the sofa surrounded by the bits of his life he'd brought with him. He stood up as she walked in. 'It happened so fast, Soph. He wanted me to carry him downstairs, but I refused. I was trying to put him down so he could slide down. I'm not used to the way he can wriggle and shift his weight. I couldn't compensate for it.'

'He can be very wriggly.' She tried for a smile. Couldn't find one.

'I shouldn't have been holding him at the top of the stairs. It wasn't just stupid; it could have been deadly. I could have killed him.'

'But you didn't. You're both a bit shocked, that's all.'

'I was taught how to go downstairs. I was taught how to fall. But not with a bairn in my arms.' He paused. Shook his head. 'I can't do this.'

Pain caught her under her ribcage. Where was this going? She didn't want to imagine. But, soul-deep, she knew. Panic had her gut twisting. 'Stuff happens, Finn. You can't always plan for everything.'

'Can't I? Don't you get it? I know what my limitations are. I know where I end and the false leg starts. I know how easy it is to lose balance. But I did it anyway. Because I wanted to hold him. Because I'm his dad and I can't get enough of him. Because I can't see further than what I want. I wanted to hold him. I wanted to feel his weight in my arms.' His eyes became dark and held little hope. 'It's not about my leg, Sophie. It's me putting myself first. Again.'

'It was an accident, Finn.'

'No. No.' She didn't want to know what was coming next. 'Doesn't that tell you I shouldn't do this?'

'Do what?' All the happiness she'd felt over the last few weeks started to dissolve. She'd been a fool to think she could find someone to love and for them to love her back. To want to stay.

Even so, she wanted to walk into his arms and hold him because she had enough belief for the both of them.

But he turned and picked up his bag. 'It's best I take a big step back here. It's all going too fast. Yeah. Maybe it'd be better if I ducked out. Obviously I'll make sure you're looked after.'

'Geez, Finn. Really? One setback and you're out?'

'I don't want to wait around for another one; it could be a lot worse.'

'We'll just be careful and put plans in place.'

What about me? She wanted to scream at him. Didn't he want to stay for her? Couldn't he make it work? For her?

'You were right all along, Soph. I can't do this. I can't be around him if I'm going to hurt him.' He closed the distance between them. Put his bag on the floor and pressed his palm to her face. 'You're amazing. And wise. And beautiful and funny.'

So stay. For me.

'Back at ya, Finn Baird.' She wanted to tell

him she loved him. The words hovered on her lips like the butterflies they'd seen together... fleeting, beautiful, ethereal...but she couldn't say them and risk him stamping on them.

But he gazed down at her and she saw the love shining there in his eyes. He was running scared, he was doing what he thought he should do. Because, whatever excuses and false truths he told himself, he had feelings for her and they went soul-deep. 'I should have listened to you in the first place, Soph. I should have stayed away.'

'I didn't know what I was talking about.' She held his wrist to keep the contact between his hand and her cheek. She didn't want to let go. 'You're very different to how I thought you'd be.'

I love you.

He shook his head. 'It was like a dream. A lovely dream where we were a family. But that's all it was. Reality is a whole different ballgame, right? Let's quit pretending it could work when there's too many reasons for it to fall apart. It's better all round if I stay away.'

The pain under her ribcage intensified. 'I know you're rattled. I know you think it's for the best—'

'It is for the best.'

He was trying to do the right thing; she got that. What he believed was right. Such was his honour and depth of feeling for his family. But while he didn't want to hurt his son, he was breaking her heart. 'Finn—'

'Mama!' Lachie's wail reached her heart and tugged. And here she was, torn between the two of them again. Torn between what she wanted and what Finn thought was best. Torn between making him stay and letting him go.

Her mothering instinct cut straight in. She could survive being heartbroken but she was not going to let Lachie suffer that. 'Finn. Do not leave. Do you hear me? If you go now then that's it. Over. You can't play this game of being in his life one minute and then not the next. It's the worst thing you could do. You're either here for good or gone for good. Okay?'

'I'm sorry, Sophie.' He picked up his bag and walked to the door.

'You're really going to do this? Break my heart? Break his?' She pointed at Lachie, who was completely oblivious to what was happening. But he wouldn't always be like that; one day he'd dream of having his father in his life. One day he'd want that more than anything else.

Finn was at the front door now. 'I am taking responsibility. For the first time in my life.'

This wasn't about the fall. It was about him not believing in himself. He still thought he was unreliable and untrustworthy. 'Families deal with things, Finn. They don't break when one thing goes wrong.'

'They do the right thing.'

'They look after each other.'

He shrugged a shoulder. 'I can't be relied upon.'

'You can say that again.' Anger pushed heartbreak out of the way but still love fluttered around the edges. Because even now she loved him—loved him for believing in his own convictions, no matter how furious they made her feel.

Fists clenched by her sides, she watched him leave but she didn't run after him and beg him to stay. Wouldn't have been able to get the words out through her closed-over throat.

He loved her, she was sure. He just didn't want to. And she was so done with loving people who didn't want to love her back.

Why the hell had she trusted him? Why had she let him into their lives and into her heart? Into Lachie's? What a fool to have been so concerned Finn would drive a wedge between her and her boy. Fool to think he wanted the same things. Fool to love him. To believe an idea of them together could be possible.

She knelt and wrapped her boy in a hug, tried not to let him see the tears landing on his coat. 'Okay. We'll be fine, little man.'

In a while. They'd build a life together and they'd be okay. It would be a wonderful life—she'd make damned sure it was—but Finn would always be there in the shadows somewhere.

Breaking her heart all over again.

'When I said let yourself fall for her I didn't mean it literally.'

'Quit the jokes, Cal. I'm not in the mood.' Why had he bothered to call his brother? Stupid idea. Finn massaged his temple. Looked out of the car window into the hospital car park. Watched the rain sluice the windscreen. *Geez*, the weather was as bad as his mood. 'You're making things worse.'

'I'm trying to get you to lighten up, Finn. So you're both okay? Apart from the bruised ego?'

'Physically. Yes.'

'So let me get this straight—you fell and you stopped Lachie from being hurt by taking the brunt of the fall yourself?'

'Uh-huh.' He'd somehow managed to twist himself to make sure Lachie had a soft landing, at a cost to his stump and his shoulder. 'The X-rays say I just have soft tissue damage. Nothing that can't be fixed by time and a wee dram.'

Unlike the heaviness in his heart. No amount of time would fix that. And alcohol would only be a temporary balm.

Loving Lachie was as natural as breathing, and he'd make sure he would always have contact and be in his life, somehow. And he could, legally, morally and emotionally: he was his father. Blood. Family. And nothing could ever change that.

The real ache in his heart was for Sophie. It had only been three hours since he'd walked away but he regretted every single step. He'd thought things would feel better once he'd made the break but they didn't. Everything felt worse.

He loved her, more than anything, but he couldn't bear to be the cause of the anguish he'd seen on her face. The blinked-away tears. The panic. The fear. Never again.

He'd been the reason she'd given up her travel plans. The reason she had to work full-time and be a single mother. He didn't want to *be* any more reasons to hurt her.

He had to protect them all, didn't he?

Cal was still talking. As was his wont. 'So you saved the boy then really? He was going to get hurt but you made sure he didn't?'

'Cal, stop. Okay? It was my fault in the first place.'

'Ach, kids get into all sorts of mischief. Adults do too, right?' Cal waved his hand. 'And we can protect them as much as we can, but sometimes stuff happens. Trust me, I know this; clearing up after stuff is my job.'

Stuff happens. Sophie had said the same. 'Stuff seems to happen a lot when I'm around.'

Cal's eyes narrowed. 'Oh? What else? And don't go mentioning the accident because we both know it was a mixture of a lot of things neither of us could have predicted.'

'I shouldn't have stepped out into nothing. I wasn't thinking straight.'

'I know.' Cal closed his eyes and looked as if he was reliving the whole episode again. 'I shouldn't have been pushing you.'

'You didn't push me.' He remembered a bit of shoving during the argument, but nothing like an intentional push over the cliff. *Hell.* His brother loved him; he knew that well enough. Not that they liked to show it.

Cal's fingers steepled on the ambulance station's white Formica table. 'I knew you were suffering, Finn. I knew you were in a bad place but I still goaded you.' His brother gave him the kind of smile he'd give to his baby daughter: tender. Tenderness from Cal Baird. It made Finn's heart clench. 'You're too hard on yourself. You want to take the blame for everything. You need to stop and look at how far you've come. Not only did you recover from the accident but you're working full-time. You love your boy enough to protect him at a cost to yourself. You want to save Sophie from hurt because that's what you think you'll give her.'

'Because I don't know if I can do anything other than that.'

'Why not?'

'Because I'm a selfish idiot.' The truth of it.

Cal nodded. 'You're talking about Mum now, and that's something else altogether.'

'How do you know?'

'I'm your brother. I know.'

If it hadn't been for Finn's stupid selfishness his son would have a grandmother to dote on him now. He had to get it out in the open, once and for all. Then Cal would understand why he'd had to back away from Sophie and Lachlan. 'I was the reason Mum had the stroke. I said I was going to go see her and I didn't. I stressed her out. I should have kept to my word, but I was all gung-ho and immature and didn't think.'

Cal shook his head and rubbed his jaw. 'Thing is, Finn, she'd had a run of small strokes before; she begged me not to tell you in case you bar-relled home and missed out on your game time.'

What the hell? 'You knew she was sick?'

'The docs said it was probably a matter of time before she had the big one, even though she was taking meds. Her blood pressure was out of control. Yes, she was sick.'

'And you kept this from me because?'

'Because we wanted you to make the most of your chances. Like I do now. Still.'

'Wait…so she was sick and you didn't tell me? How could you do that?' His mind went off at a tangent. If his brother had told him their mother was sick he'd have made sure to visit her. If his mum hadn't died he wouldn't have been so hard on himself, wouldn't have fallen into a bad run of form in his rugby, wouldn't have met Sophie.

So many ifs.

'I'm sorry. I didn't realise you'd taken it so much to heart and blamed yourself. You have a huge capacity to love people, Finn. You've just got to believe in it.' Cal leaned forward, made sure to make eye contact. 'Do you love this woman?'

Whoa, back to Sophie again. He didn't hesitate. 'Yes. Absolutely.'

'Do you want to make a go of it with her?' Cal paused for a beat then added, 'I don't want a speech or justification of why you can't. Do you *want* to? Just yes or no will do.'

Again, no hesitation. 'Yes.' More than anything.

'Assuming she wants you. And I have to say she needs her head checking on that score. But...' Cal grinned '...you have a chance to have a family, Finn. Don't stuff it up. Go back and tell her you're sorry and you're going to make it work. Or I will.'

'You wouldn't? Please back off from my life, Cal.'

His brother laughed. 'As soon as you stop stuffing it up I'll back right off. Okay? I don't want to see your sad ugly face here again until you have good news.'

'I'm a grown man with a son. I have a responsible job and a heap of sporting medals. Will there ever be a time when you're going to treat me as your equal and not your baby brother?'

'I doubt it.' Cal shrugged in the way annoying siblings did. 'So deal with it.'

Looked like he was going to have to. And he was going to deal with the Sophie situation. Right now.

* * *

Sophie checked her phone for the millionth time. No messages. No missed calls. Nothing.

Although she didn't know why she was torturing herself by checking. He wasn't going to phone. He'd been determined to leave.

Cursing, she threw the phone down next to her on the couch and flicked through the TV channels. Nothing worth her attention there either.

She picked up her phone again. Dialled. Breathed out when the call was answered. 'Hannah. Hey. Yes, I'm fine. He's fine. Listen… I need a distraction—tell me about that hen night you went on last Saturday.' When Sophie had been comatose and Finn had looked after her. Pain hit her in the chest. When would she stop thinking about him? 'Fun?'

'As ever. And so much gossip.' Hannah paused.

'Spill the beans.' *Make my thoughts stop.*

Her friend coughed. 'You want me to talk you down, right? Has he rung?' The best thing about friends was that they didn't mind when you called them at work and cried your eyes out. They took you out for lunch and made sure you ate something. And they listened for the nth time about your fractured love life.

'No. No calls. No texts.' And he'd only left this morning. Nowhere near enough time for either of them to gather their thoughts properly. All she knew was that she ached to see him, to hold him. And that that ache wouldn't go away for a very long time. 'It's been a crappy day.'

'If I ever see him can I personally tell him what I think?'

'No. Yes.' Sophie smiled. She had people she loved and who loved her; she was glad of that. Somehow they'd pull her through this. 'Okay, Rottweiler. You can do your worst.' Which was fairly bad; Sophie had seen her in action before.

A sharp knock on the door made her jump—made her heart jump too. 'Er…there's someone at the door.'

'Is it him? Quick, go look. Through the curtains or something.' Hannah breathed heavily. 'If it is, pass the phone over to me so I get my chance.'

Sophie dragged herself from the sofa and to the front door; her body ached from the wonderful things he'd done to her last night. She didn't want that particular ache to ever go. 'It'll be someone selling something; it always is.' She pulled the door open and froze. 'Oh.'

'Is it him?'

'Yes.' Rain dripped from his hair, flattening it to his head. Little rivulets ran down his cheeks, over his nose. His eyes sparked determination and so many other emotions it made her dizzy to see them. Because they were all directed at her: love, fear, passion. 'Finally found something to tame the Baird hair, then?'

He ran his hand over his wet head. 'I don't want anything tamed when I'm around you.'

What did that mean? She wasn't going to allow herself to hope. 'Did you forget something? Why are you here?'

'Can I talk to him?' She'd forgotten Hannah was on speaker phone. Her voice was loud and piercing.

He took the phone out of Sophie's hand. 'This is Finn.'

'I hope you're pleased with yourself? That's twice you've hurt her. She's a sweet, lovely woman and she deserves better than you.'

He looked at Sophie again. Captured her heart

with his gaze. 'I know she does. Oh, and you forgot sexy. She's sexy and clever and funny. And I love her.'

'Sorry, Hannah, got to go.' He *what?* Sophie grabbed the phone and clicked it off. Stepped aside to let him in out of the rain, even though he deserved to be in it for a good time longer. Then she hauled up some of her friend's inner Rottweiler. 'You can't come here and say things you don't mean.'

'I mean every word.' He took her hand. 'I stuffed up, Sophie. I hurt you and I'm so sorry. I realised that by walking away I was making everything ten times worse. It's not about my leg, is it? It's not actually about dropping Lachie, in the end, because a man with two legs could do that—that was just an accident. It's about believing in myself—in my heart and my love for you. It's about knowing I will do the right thing and choose you two before me, every time.'

'Damned right it is. I was willing to do that for you.' But then she'd always chased the love she couldn't have.

'When I walked away from you I was putting myself first. I was choosing not to work with you to find answers and solutions. That was beyond selfish. I was being Billy and choosing to go for a pint instead of finding help.'

'But you can't yoyo in and out of our lives, Finn. It's not fair. You have to be sure and you have to stay.'

'I know.' He was starting to shiver from cold. His hand shook as he smoothed down her hair. She felt love in his touch, in the way he looked at her. 'I know you waited for your parents to come home. I know you packed your suitcase and cried when they didn't come. I can't be that person who does that to either of you.'

'But you did it already.'

He closed his eyes, took a breath. 'Sometimes it's overwhelming. All of this. You. Lachie. Being a father. Being an amputee. I got lost in it all. I'm so sorry, Sophie. So sorry. I won't get lost again. I want to stay here with you, my anchor, my everything.'

Hope bloomed in her chest, in her heart. He understood her. He understood himself and that was most of the battle. With that they could move forward. They could love. She stepped close to him, wrapped her arms around him, felt the steady beat of his heart, his strength. Strength he hadn't known he'd had until he was tested. And tested again. This man had been through so much and survived, and she loved him for that with every cell in her body. 'If you start to lose your way, just say so, Finn. Let me help you. I want to do that…not because I don't think you can manage, but because we're a team. Believe me, there will be days I need to lean on you too.'

'Any time. All the time. Every day, Sophie. I don't want to be apart from you and Lachie ever again.' He reached into his pocket and pulled out a box. Then he was letting go of her and kneeling down. It wasn't a pretty kneel but it was a beautiful Finn one. 'Sophie, will you forgive me? I love you. Will you make a family with me? Marry me?'

Tears pricked and she didn't fight them. She was done with trying not to love him. All she could see was a man who had captured her heart and her soul, who made her happy, who made her world complete. And a beautiful ring that signified his love for her. Their love. 'Yes. Yes, of course. I love you too. So much.'

She kind of wished she'd kept Hannah on the phone for that bit.

But then he was standing up and hauling her to him and kissing her as if his world was complete too. When he pulled away he was breathless and shining. 'You know what makes me sad the most?'

'What's that?' She didn't want to think of him being sad.

'If I hadn't been like this I could have loved you longer. Both of you.'

'Well, today is the beginning of the rest of our lives. We just have to love harder from now on to make up for it.' She tugged his damp shirt from his pants, laughing at the quick upturn of his mouth. Loving the feel of him against her. Loving him. 'If you don't want to get sick we need to get you out of these wet things super quick.'

'Yes please.' He kissed her again. And again. 'If you insist.'

EPILOGUE

Twelve months later

'DADDY! DADDY, COME and see the big boat!' Lachie ran back along the lakeside path towards Finn, grabbed his hand and tugged him to see the great old-fashioned steamboat on Lake Wakatipu. A warm summer breeze caught up the boy's hair, tugging his curls in every direction.

Daddy. That never got old. Finn picked up his boy and swung him onto his shoulders so he could better see the deep blue lake and the fancy boat and steam. 'Look at that! And see the ducks there.'

'Whoa! Careful.' Cal frowned at him the way big brothers did and reached a hand to Lachie's back to steady him. 'Sure you're okay doing that move?'

Irritation rankled, but Finn forced it back. Time here was short and he wasn't going to let old arguments bite. 'It's fine. I've perfected it. We know exactly how to do it, right, Lachie?'

'Yes, Daddy. I have to stay very still.' His foot rocked against Finn's heart, stamping on it little impressions of love. 'We can do it 'cos we're a team.'

'Never thought I'd see the day you were settled. But you're full of surprises, Finn.' Cal's hand had left Lachie's back and was now clamped on Finn's shoulder, making Finn's chest contract unexpectedly. 'I think it's time I backed off the bossy bit now. You're on your own.' He laughed. 'But if you need me—'

'I know.' Finn exhaled. 'But thanks, anyway. You were a great stand-in dad, even though you should never have been put in that position in the first place.' He owed Cal so much. One visit to the other side of the world was not going to be enough to pay him back.

Lachie tugged on Finn's hair and giggled. 'Where's Mummy?'

Finn turned and caught sight of Sophie, swinging little Grace between her and Cal's wife, Abbie. She looked up and saw him watching her and she waved, her mouth forming the words, *Thank you.*

He hung back a little and waited for them to catch up. Managed to get her to himself for one minute. 'Thank you for what?'

'For bringing me here to New Zealand. For helping me live my dreams of travel. For loving me.' She snuggled against him, caught Lachie's foot in her hand. 'Before it's all too difficult.'

Finn pressed his hand to the tiny belly she was growing. A new life. He couldn't believe he could be this lucky. 'Life will never be difficult. Not with you. Did I ever tell you how much I love you?'

'Yes. Every day. At least three million times.' She stood on tiptoe and kissed him. 'Don't ever stop.'

'Not a chance.' And then he told her again, just to make sure she knew.

* * * * *

LET'S TALK
Romance

For exclusive extracts, competitions
and special offers, find us online:

 facebook.com/millsandboon

 @millsandboonuk

 @millsandboon

Or get in touch on 0844 844 1351*

For all the latest titles coming soon,
visit millsandboon.co.uk/nextmonth

*Calls cost 7p per minute plus your phone company's price per
minute access charge

Want even more
ROMANCE?

Join our bookclub today!

'Mills & Boon books, the perfect way to escape for an hour or so.'

Miss W. Dyer

'Excellent service, promptly delivered and very good subscription choices.'

Miss A. Pearson

'You get fantastic special offers and the chance to get books before they hit the shops'

Mrs V. Hall

Visit millsandbook.co.uk/Bookclub and save on brand new books.

MILLS & BOON